The Battle-ax People

Beginnings of Western Culture

ALSO BY OLIVIA VLAHOS

Human Beginnings
African Beginnings

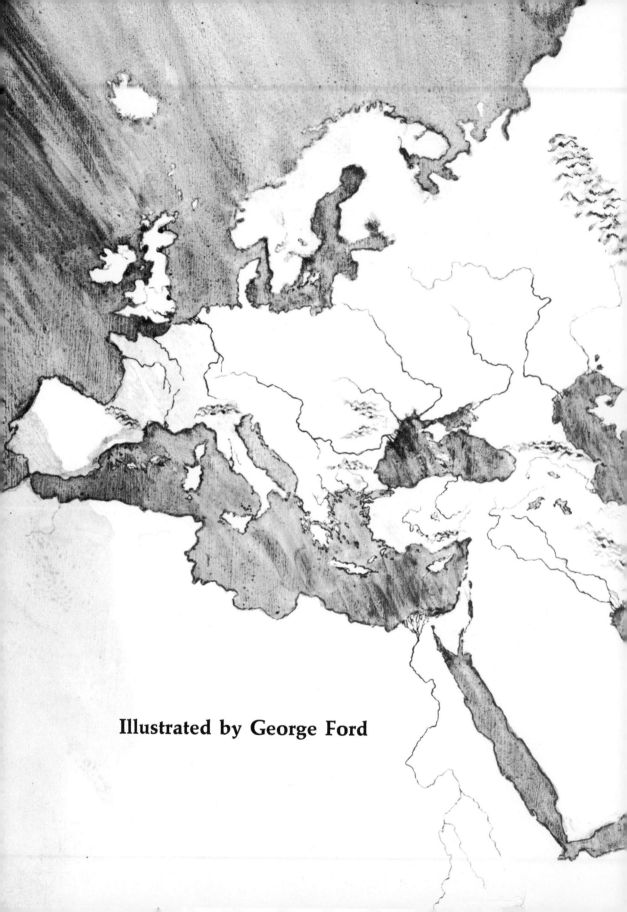

Illustrated by George Ford

OLIVIA VLAHOS

The Battle-ax People

Beginnings of Western Culture

THE VIKING PRESS   NEW YORK

For Melissa and Stephanie—
two who have "inherited" English
for a native language, and Western
civilization for a way of life

Copyright © 1968 by Olivia Vlahos
All rights reserved
First published in 1968 by The Viking Press, Inc.
625 Madison Avenue, New York, N.Y. 10022
Published simultaneously in Canada by
The Macmillan Company of Canada Limited
Library of Congress catalog card number: 68–30743
Printed in U.S.A. by Halliday Lithograph

913   1. Prehistoric and historic archaeology
901   1. Ancient civilizations
572   1. Cultural and linguistic anthropology

Acknowledgments

Culture travels by many roads, changing as it goes, evolving, adding new ideas, and acquiring different dimensions. And so this tale of the barbarian Battle-ax People and their kin, our language ancestors, is as much a tale of things learned as of things begun. It is meant to convey an impression of ancient history and its bearing on Western civilization rather than hard history itself. If the reader finds in these pages a useful frame in which to put more detailed facts, I shall be content.

The research on which the book is based has been drawn primarily from the archaeological record and from the writings of specialists in Indo-European languages. Overview works by Vere Gordon Childe, Stuart Piggott, and Hugh Hencken have given orientation. In all studies having to do with the nature of man and with his dim past, there are many ambiguities and areas of scientific controversy. I confess to having skimped archaeology's uncertainties in favor of its sometimes tentative conclusions. Tomorrow's new evidence may well require different evaluations, and the reader will want to keep this in mind.

This is the third book of mine which has been shepherded into print by Beatrice Rosenfeld, Science Editor of The Viking Press. Her taste and discernment, her enthusiasm and eagle eye for detail have added to and vastly improved them all. For this the reader will surely be as grateful as I am.

Contents

Prologue   13
Our Language Ancestors

PART I: INTO OLD LANDS, AMONG CITY FOLK

1.   Kassites   31
      Conquerors of Babylon

2.   Hittites   47
      Governing in Anatolia

3.   Mitanni   61
      A Kingdom of Charioteers

4.   Hyksos   73
      Freebooting in Egypt

5.   Aryans   89
      Swallowed Up in India

6.   Persians   105
      A Meeting of Minds

PART II: MOVING WEST

7. Minoans and Mycenaeans   121
    Something New in Europe

8. Golden Greece   135
    The Flowering

9. Rome   149
    The Propagation

10. Celts and Their Precursors   165
    Settling Europe

11. Teutons, Sarmatians, and Vikings   179
    The Final Waves

Epilogue   194
    A Capsule History of the English Language

Chronology   206
Bibliography   209
Index   219

List of Maps and Charts

Maximum Extent of European Ice Sheet During Last Ice Age   12
Migrations of the Battle-ax People   19
Chart of Familiar Words in Indo-European Languages   23
Indo-European Family Tree   25
Mesopotamia   34
The Hittite Empire   49
The Mitanni in the Middle East   65
Ancient Egypt   78
Aryan Invasions of India   94
Persian Empire about 500 B.C.   109
The Minoan-Mycenaean World   124
Greek Settlements in the Seventh Century B.C.   141
Early Rome   151
Roman Empire During the Reign of Trajan (98–117 A.D.)   157
Spread of Urnfield Culture   170

The Battle-ax People

Beginnings of Western Culture

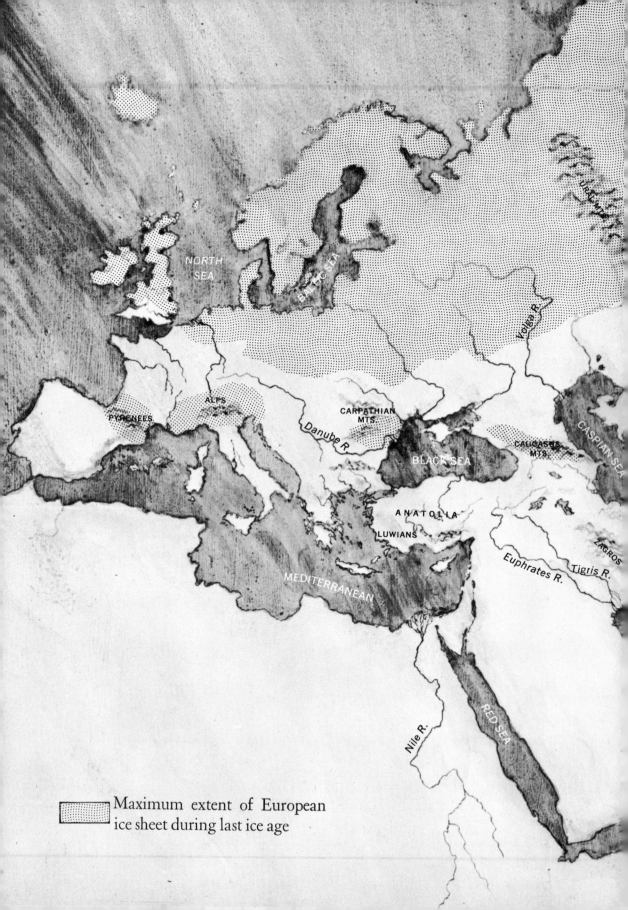

NORTH
SEA

BALTIC SEA

URAL MTS.

Volga R.

CARPATHIAN
MTS.

CAUCASUS
MTS.

CASPIAN SEA

ALPS

PYRENEES

Danube R.

BLACK SEA

ANATOLIA

LUWIANS

ZAGROS

Euphrates R.

Tigris R.

MEDITERRANEAN

Nile R.

RED SEA

Maximum extent of European
ice sheet during last ice age

Prologue

Our Language Ancestors

At the end of the last ice age, ten thousand years ago, when the glacier had melted away from what is now Europe, people moved in to take possession of the newly uncovered land. It was a land clothed in some places in thick forests of oak and ash. In some places there were vast meadowlands—plains of grass stretching as far as the eye could see.

The early hunting people who had always lived on the edge of the glacier spread out and continued their way of life. Some, perhaps much like the Eskimos of today, had grown so accustomed to the harsh life of winter that they followed the snow—or the animals that lived in it. Some continued to track game along ancient trails, setting up their portable shelters of bark or skin wherever the hunting was good. Some settled permanently on the edges of lakes and seas, hunting now and then but living primarily on the fruit of the waters—seals and fish and shellfish. Eventually their villages were built on mounds of discarded shells.

Far to the south in lands we now call Turkey, Iran, and Iraq, people had already learned to grow their food. Gradually the farming idea spread. It spread with the farmers themselves, forever in search of new soil to till when the old fields would bear no more. In time farmers moved into what is now Europe, following the Danube River into the new land. They reached Scandinavia and crossed the narrow channel—newly formed as glacial ice melted—to occupy the British Isles. Everywhere they mingled in friendly fashion with the earlier hunting and fishing folk. And why not? Their numbers were few— at least in the beginning. They neither disturbed the game nor even made much of a dent in the forest. Practicing a slash-and-burn method of clearing their fields, these early farmers would hack out a piece of woodland, build a village, and then after a few years move on, leaving their empty houses and the graves of their dead behind, slowly to be obliterated by the patient trees. Sometimes they built community graves of stone and earth, graves in which all the dead of a village could sleep, and these have defeated the encroachments of forest and time to be revealed to us by the archaeologist's spade.

Over on the far side of the Danube other sorts of people lived. Their land supported no dense forests. It was instead a vast plain—some of it dry steppe, some of it a sea of grass. From the Carpathian Mountains in central Europe to the borders of China this great plain spread. It was—and is—a land on the whole better suited to stock raising than to farming, and by 3000 B.C. that is what most of the plainsmen were doing there. They must have been a mixed lot, those plainsmen, even as they are today, speaking a variety of tongues and wearing a variety of faces—some slant-eyed and black-haired, some blue-eyed and fair-haired, with every variation in between. They seem to have shared common interests and habits, however, and certainly a common way of life. The most westerly of these ancient herdsmen hold particular interest for us of the Western world because we think they may have been our language ancestors. That is, the language they spoke was probably the grandparent tongue from which English, much, much later, developed. And not English alone, but also Latin and Greek,

French, German, Russian—nearly all the languages of Europe, in fact, as well as those of Iran and of many parts of India. Wherever these western herdsmen traveled from their homeland (somewhere just north of the Caucasus Mountains seems the likeliest spot), they took their language with them. And now, because of its wide geographical spread, the grandparent language is called Indo-European, and all its descendants belong to the Indo-European family.

What the grandparent people themselves called their language we shall never know. They had no writing to perpetuate the name. All we know about them has been learned, first from a comparison of certain words which appear in similar form in all the daughter languages, and then from a careful study of the burials of these people.

Over a span of two thousand years in time and more than that many miles in space the graves of these people and their descendent tribes were made in much the same way. Sometimes the graves contained great riches, sometimes not, but always they were similar in type and in furnishings. Plains people and their descendants—wherever they roamed—were laid to rest in single graves heaped over with great barrows of earth. Graves of chieftains were particularly imposing in barrow size and particularly well equipped within. A mortuary house of wood or stone sheltered the chief's body, and in surrounding chambers were placed the bodies of servants, bodyguards, and certainly a wife or two, all carefully arranged so that they could hear the chief's ghostly voice and rise to serve him. Horses, oxen, and perhaps a dog were also dispatched to accompany their master. The cart or wagon that had borne the chiefly body to its grave was dismantled and placed in the burial chamber. There, too, were stacked pots and jars made to look as if cords had been wrapped around the rims. Ornaments and standards of various kinds were included. Close to the chief's hand was laid a selection of weapons, including always a shaft-hole ax made of metal if possible, otherwise of stone. These mighty axes seem to have been a special mark of distinction, and so invariably do they appear in barrow graves that scholars call their owners the Battle-ax People.

Now these people were exactly what you might expect of semi-nomadic, tribal folk. They were warlike, because herders' wealth is movable wealth, an open invitation to enemy raiders. (You might compare them very roughly to American Plains Indians with their horse herds. Like these Indians, some Battle-ax folk even lived in tepees made of felt and took enemy scalps for trophies.) Certainly they all admired courage and strength, and their heroes were warriors whose deeds were celebrated by bards.

Deities of later plainsmen were occasionally earth goddesses—like those of the planting people—but the more ancient groups seem to have preferred father gods, sky gods, thunderers, keepers of the light-ning and the rain. One word did duty for "divinity," "day," "lumi-nous sky," and "Heaven"—an affinity to be preserved in both Latin (*deus,* god; *dies,* day) and Greek. In Sanskrit, an ancient Indo-Eu-ropean language of India, the sky god—the sky itself—is named Dyaus-Pitr, Father of Heaven, which has its echo in the Latin Diespiter (eventually Jupiter), in the Greek Zeus-Pater, and in the Teutonic Ziu. In later Indian times, the father was slowly overshadowed by his celestial sons and then forgotten altogether, a common fate of gods.

Indo-European gods often seem to have been grouped in male triads to cover various divine virtues or to personify certain aspects of nature. So we find Indra–Mitra–Varuna in India and Zeus–Ares–Posei-don in Greece. In the north were Ziu (Tiw)–Woden–Thor—whence come our Tuesday, Wednesday, and Thursday every week of the year. Symbols of the sun—circles and spirals—seem to have been important to these people, too, though whether such figures were their own invention or had been borrowed from various settled peoples along the line of march no one can say.

Having once been hunters, they continued to hunt for sport in between raids and war, and some of the old hunting symbols remained in their artistic vocabulary. Animal emblems of all kinds appear in their richest graves—stags and horses and cattle figures. Sometimes they favored images of gods or shamans which were part stag, part man. In the art of the Scythians—latter-day plainsmen whom the Greeks of 500 B.C. knew and described—the animal figures became fantasy figures of such beautiful and curious form that they inspired countless imitations and somehow worked their way into the heraldry of medieval Europe.

Sometime before 3000 B.C. the Battle-ax people began to trade with the outposts of civilization on the other side of the Caucasus. At these centers they learned to cast their battle-axes in copper and later in bronze. Down near the Persian Gulf where the Tigris and Euphrates rivers meet the sea, Sumerian city folk had earlier than 3000 B.C. used wheeled vehicles yoked to oxen and onagers, small asses native to the region. Whether the Battle-ax People simply took the Sumerian lesson to heart or whether (as archaeologist Stuart Piggott suggests) they and the Sumerians as well had borrowed from inventors who lived just south of the Caucasus—or whether they themselves originated the idea—is something we may never know. However the Battle-ax People did acquire their knowledge of the wheel, they put it to wide use soon after 3000 B.C. Their carts and wagons were hitched first to oxen and then to horses. The horse, once hunted and herded, was now harnessed and sometimes even venerated.

The Battle-ax People began to move. Not in a great wave at first, but in warrior groups and in family groups traveling in solid-wheeled wagons. Perhaps their homeland was growing crowded; perhaps there was less rain than usual and meager forage for the herds. Whatever the reason, the great move was on in earnest.

Sometime before 2000 B.C. one such group came down into Anatolia (now modern Turkey). Whether it was by way of the Caucasus Mountains or around the Black Sea we do not know. Picking up ideas and luxury items from the civilized folk around them, they grew and prospered. The rich graves of their chieftains testify to that. Battle-axes, standards, animal figures—all were cast in copper and gold.

Later, other Battle-ax tribes swept over the Caucasus into Anatolia, overwhelming those of their own people already in residence as well as the local civilized folk. They adopted the planting gods of the land and the Mesopotamian way of writing and eventually built up a vast empire that would one day challenge Egypt. They became known to history as the Hittites.

At some point in their Middle Eastern travels, Battle-ax warriors invented the light, maneuverable battle cart with spoked wheels and became the first charioteers. With their new skills and equipment they must have been much sought after as mercenary soldiers, or perhaps they simply overawed the local folk among whom they appeared. In any case, one contingent of Battle-ax charioteers seems to have led into Egypt an army of desert folk (the combined force known to us as the Hyksos). Their conquest of that old and somewhat backward kingdom at least delivered the wheel to people who, up to that time, had had to make do with boats for travel, sledges for construction work, and human foot power in war.

Another group of Battle-ax warriors—the Kassites—led an army of hillmen against Babylonia and ended the dynasty founded by Hammurabi. Still others of these freebooting charioteers carved out their own kingdom in what is now northern Syria and called it Mitanni.

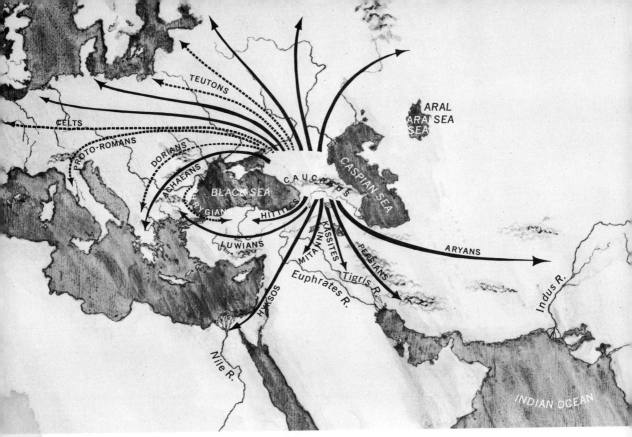

Migrations of the Battle-ax People
—— First Wave
---- Later Waves

From the Iranian Plateau Battle-ax People called the Aryans moved into India. With their coming, civilization in that land disappeared, not to return until the Aryans were themselves tamed to civilized ways. Greece was invaded by a Battle-ax people called the Achaeans, future heroes of the Trojan War. Into Italy migrated the Battle-ax ancestors of the Romans, and into Scandinavia went the precursors of the Vikings, battle-axes in hand, joyfully taking to boats even in those early times.

For a time all these wanderers must have retained vague memories of their ancestral home north of the Caucasus, of the wide plains and wider skies and mountains far in the distance. But as the miles between the groups lengthened, as they lost contact with one another, their memories faded, their languages changed form, and they adopted the customs of the peoples they had conquered.

This was particularly true in the Middle East, where city life and city learning were far richer and more complex, far more imposing than anything the warrior plainsmen had ever known. In Europe proper, however, some interesting amalgams took place. These are preserved to this day in old European myths celebrating the divine marriages of sky gods and earth goddesses. The struggles that preceded the celestial marriages are also preserved in tales of warrior heroes who bravely conquer great snakes or dragons—the fertility symbols of the planting folk. Sometimes the new combinations of people and ideas were given permanent art forms in carvings or castings which displayed cult figures of the farmers, the herders, even the vanishing hunters with marvelous impartiality.

The Battle-ax People who remained behind on the plains continued to expand. No matter how many emigrants went out, the original grazing grounds never seemed to be sufficient for the need. The westtern grasslands were always more lush than those of the east, and a drought anywhere on the Central Asian plains sent tribe after tribe bouncing against one another as they sought and fought for better pastures.

On the whole, plainsmen were a conservative lot in terms of new ideas, but even the stay-at-homes changed a little from time to time. For one thing, they took to riding their horses instead of harnessing them to chariots. And with the newfangled notion of riding astride came a newfangled article of dress—or at least a renewed version of an older tailored garment. The new item was trousers. It was a fad to be widely copied. Beginning on the Iranian Plateau, pants traveled across the Caucasus to the men of the steppes beyond and on into Europe with the Celts. The Greeks were to reject the new style out

of hand. The Romans would also resist until forays into colder climes brought on so many chilblained knees that a sort of knicker suit was devised for Roman soldiers.

Continuously the plains people pushed against the civilized settlements to the south and west, starting new waves of conquest and migration rolling over their former brethren. Around 1200 B.C. the Indo-European Phrygians (a warrior folk originating somewhere near the Black Sea) invaded Anatolia and brought down the powerful Hittites. Related groups called the Sea People challenged mighty Egypt, and occupied the Syrian coast at the same time that Joshua and his Hebrew flock, newly released from bondage, were pushing into the same area. The Greek-speaking Dorians overran the Greek-speaking Achaeans, bringing a dark age to the Aegean. And the Celts, an Indo-European people who had settled along the Danube and fallen heir to farm ways and the forging of iron, were pushed out by tribes behind them. They then began a slow procession across Europe that was to take them eventually to Gaul and to Britain, in both places to suffer defeat at the hands of Roman legions. Among the last of the Battle-ax People were the Teutons, who were to be parents of our own English and whose final push would crumble the walls of great Rome herself.

The languages spoken by all these people had grown from a single grandparent tongue spoken in a great grassland between two seas, bounded by a mountain wall. Its earliest written samples occur in Hittite cuneiform and in Sanskrit hymns from India. And even these languages were descendants which had grown away somewhat from the original. Scholars have, nevertheless, learned a great deal about the old Indo-European prototype by studying those words which occur in similar form in all the related languages. What sorts of words would those be? The ones which are closest to the heart and change the least. Family words, very often, home words, words which have to do with everyday life.

	MOTHER	FATHER	BROTHER	SISTER	EAT	WATER
SANSKRIT	Mata	Pita	Bhratr	Svasar	Admi	Udan
HITTITE		Attas			Et-, Ez-	Watar
GERMAN	Mutter	Vater	Bruder	Schwester	Essen	Wasser
GREEK	Meter	Pater	Phrater	Heor	Edein	Hydor
LATIN	Mater	Pater	Frater	Soror	Edere	(W)Aqua
FRENCH	Mère	Père	Frère	Soeur	[Manger]	Eau
SPANISH	Madre	Padre	[Hermano]	[Hermana]	Comer (Cum-edo)	Agua
OLD IRISH	Mathair	Athir	Bhrathair	Siur	Ithim	Uisque
RUSSIAN	Mat	[Oyets]	Brat	Sestra	Yest	Voda
POSSIBLE INDO-EURO-PEAN ROOT	Mater	Pater	Bhrater	Swesor	Ed	Aw-Awer

They learned, too, that in these words certain regular sound-changes occur, quite predictably. The initial *p* sound in Sanskrit, for example, while remaining the same in Greek, Latin, and Slavic, changes to *f* in the Germanic languages, to *h* in Armenian, and in Celtic is simply dispensed with altogether. You can check this change through in the words for "father." By taking into account the expected sound-changes in a word as it moves from language to language, the ancient root word can often be uncovered. Sometimes the trail is muddled by the substitution of slang words or by semantic changes which obscure the root. The root for "brother," for example, which remains fairly constant through all the related languages (only a few appear on the chart above), is dropped entirely in Spanish. The Spanish use instead *hermano,* which comes from the Latin *germanus,* meaning cousin or relative. In Spanish the *bhratr–frater* root found expression in the word *fray,* which means a brother in the Church.

The use of the same root in different ways results in some curious language couples. One such pair is *anchor–ankle.* Both derive from an ancient Indo-European root meaning "to bend." In one language the bend was seen in a boat anchor; in another it applied to the bend of the human foot. Both terms made their way into English.

By studying the words which have survived in similar though somewhat changed form in all the Indo-European languages, it is possible to get a fair idea of what the early Battle-ax People were like. We know, for instance, that they did *not* originate in a tropical climate. All the descendants have similar words for snow, bear, wolf, pine tree. They have no similar words for palm tree, rhinoceros, or elephant.

We know something of the plainsmen's arsenal. All the language descendants have similar words for ax, bow, arrow, javelin, spear, and sword. We know that metals were important to them: similar words exist for gold, silver, and copper. The root for copper is an all-purpose term often used for bronze and iron as well. Its ultimate origin as well as that of the word for ax is said to be traceable to Sumer. Not surprising when you recall where and how the Battle-ax People learned their metallurgy.

When it comes to transport, the words cluster in heaps. All Indo-European daughter languages have similar words for axle, hub, and yoke (but not spoke). And as for wheels, there are two complete groups. In Latin there is *rota;* in Irish, *roth;* in Old German, *rad;* in Sanskrit, *ratha;* in Persian, *ratho;* and in modern Greek, *roda*—all of which anciently meant chariot as well as wheel. But there are also *cakram* in Sanskrit, *kyklos* in Greek, *kolo* in Old Saxon, and *hweol* in Anglo-Saxon, whence comes the English *wheel.*

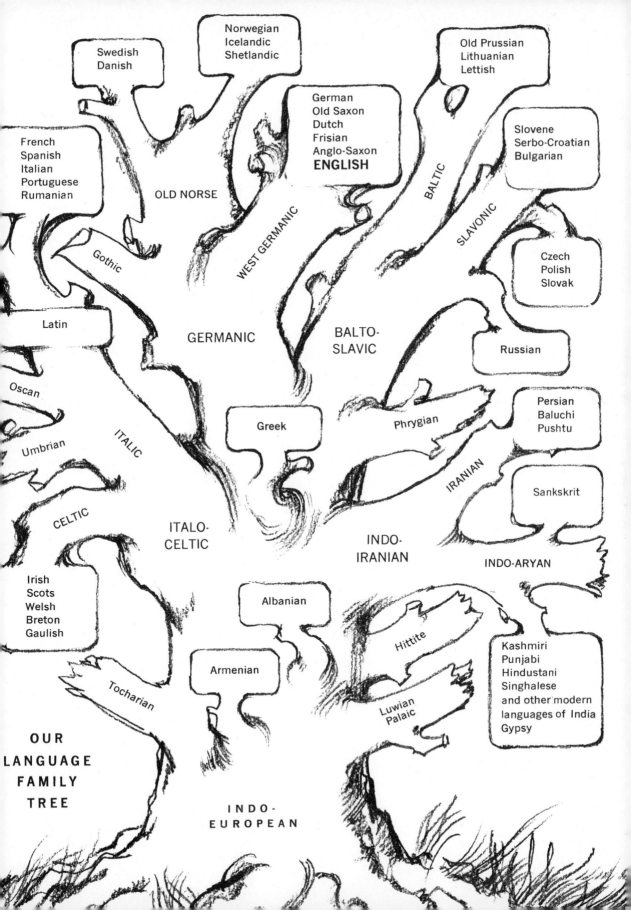

Surviving roots tell us that the Battle-ax people knew a lot about stock raising, though probably not a great deal about farming. There are common words for cattle, sheep, horses and their breeding, and for dairy products. The Battle-ax People seem to have recognized only three seasons: a cold period, spring, and a hot summer. There exists no common root in the related languages for harvesttime. There are, however, common roots for the words for plow, grain, and farmer, too, though this applies, as often as not, to the herdsman rather than the tiller of soil. Some specialists have taken the existence of these common roots to mean that the Battle-ax People were settled farmers first and wandering stockmen afterward, not hunters turned herders as others have supposed.

However the early Battle-ax People came to the herding way of life, they certainly made of it something quite different in every respect from the way of life of neighboring farmers in southern Russia. Whether men of the Battle-ax tribes had ever farmed or whether they had simply made it woman's work (as herding people of Africa do even today), their descendants in time came to loathe farming and to scorn farming folk. In the fifth century B.C., the Greek historian Herodotus was to say that among the nomadic tribes called the Thracians, "to be idle is accounted the most honorable thing, and to be a tiller of the ground the most dishonorable. To live by war and plunder is of all things the most glorious." The Scythian tribesmen he called "mare-milkers . . . who neither plow nor sow." In Caesar's time, Roman historians were still describing "wagon-dwellers and nomads" who subsisted on meat and milk from their herds and on tribute grain received from local farmers who tilled their land. Anywhere and everywhere the plainsman's way of life seems to include a scorn of settled folk. Television Westerns preserve for us the classic conflict between cattlemen and "sodbusters." Even today in the Lake

Balkhash region of Russia there live the remnants of Genghis Khan's motley and mighty Mongol horde. They are still, as always, herders, moving seasonally with their stock, still aloof from farmers and farming, dependent for their grain on peasants who come from other ethnic groups.

As to the family life and tribal life of the early Battle-ax People, surviving root words cannot tell us much, though some specialists claim otherwise. Judging by the old historical comments, however, we could guess that the plainsmen probably had a male-dominated society as do most herding peoples everywhere. It is worth noting the single exception we know of. In one of the later Central Asian hordes, maidens were allowed to accompany warriors into battle. And not only did they accompany, they fought as well. Indeed they had to or risk spinsterhood, for no girl could marry until she had personally slain a foe. This curious custom and these warrior-maidens survive in Greek myth as the Amazons.

We can suppose that, like hunting and herding people anywhere (cowboys and cattle rustlers of the American West, for that matter), early Battle-ax men were rugged individualists. They had to be in order to survive. They must also have been fiercely loyal to strong leaders and quick to obey, for in their hazardous world, good leadership was another condition of survival. And indeed, great honors were paid to dead chieftains, and enormous barrows were raised in their memory. In time the rights to the chieftaincy must have become hereditary in a certain family of every tribe. From this family was chosen the man most fit to rule. Perhaps that family and the chief's personal guard or companions became in time a kind of aristocracy—an aristocracy in which honor could be validated only in cattle, in battle, and in birth. (Until recent times there was still a reflection of such class distinctions among the Turkic-speaking Kazakh Balkhash, who divided their people into "white bones" and "black bones": rich nobles descended from Genghis Khan and poor commoners.)

In their long wanderings the Battle-ax People may well have left behind something more than a change of language. On the face of Europe they stamped the indelible features of the warrior. Their ideas of the proper sort of family and the proper occupations for a man to follow and the proper, the honorable ways for a man to live come down to us, not only through Roman law, but in all the fairy tales of our childhood. For these were, in their beginnings, myths and legends of the Battle-ax People, which, with new rule and new religions, took refuge in the nursery.

Because of the Battle-ax People, admiration for horses became engrained in the ways of Europeans. In any Indo-European language the words which describe honorable conduct and a noble gentleman carry also the meaning "horseman." The Greek *hippobotes,* the English *cavalier,* the Latin *equites,* the French *chevalier,* the German *ritter,* and the Spanish *caballero* are some of them. In the current Western passion for the automobile we can perhaps see a simple switch in honor-object from horse to machine.

From earliest times the Battle-ax People were rovers. Was it a lingering echo of this restlessness that sent European explorers sailing around the globe and sends men today out beyond the globe and into space? If so, then perhaps it is fitting that one group of the new wanderers sets out on its cosmic journeys from the plains of southern Russia where the Battle-ax People began.

Part I

INTO OLD LANDS,

AMONG CITY FOLK

1. Kassites

Conquerors of Babylon

It is early morning. The sun rising behind the mountain peaks throws dark shadows into hidden valleys, across tiny lakes. Up out of the shadows and into the rocky passage between two hills moves a small group of men. They are tall and fair. Some of them are dressed in short trousers of cowhide fastened here and there with horn buttons. Others wear kilts of woven cloth. Most are young, barely out of boyhood, and they swagger boldly, importantly, under the eyes of the bearded veterans who lead them. But this is no band of revelers out for a stroll. This is a raiding party, and the men, young or old, are warriors. Over their shoulders are short bows made of glued horn, and slung at their belts, ready to hand, are battle-axes of metal or stone.

The leaders are trying to maintain a decent quiet as befits their mission. Impossible. The clattering hoofs of the horses, the neighing, the frantic rearing and snorting when an animal sights a snake—all this announces the approach of the raiders as surely as a brazen trumpet blast. Worst of all is the creaking cart. Clearly it is unsuited for use in hill country. Its heavy, solid wheels are forever being jolted off their axle, thereby causing much delay and hard labor. The cart must be pushed as well as pulled up steep slopes and held back on the downgrade by men sliding along helplessly on their heels. But it is, all the same, a necessary item. Necessary for group prestige and necessary to hold the plunder of a dozen raided villages.

It also holds one boy, wounded as they attacked the fierce little hillmen at the last village but one. He has been made as comfortable as possible, but his torn arm throbs painfully every time the cart wheels jolt over another stone. He presses his lips together tightly, determined to let no cry escape them, for this time of wandering and raiding into far countries is the warrior's test of fitness. And he badly wants to be a warrior, to be admired and deferred to by the women and younger boys. Try as he will, though, he cannot control his thoughts. They wander, as fever fancies will, back to the wide plains beyond the mountains, to the felt tents of his own clan, to his mother with her cool hands and soft voice. When, when will this wandering be done . . .

The Battle-ax People could have moved south and west in this way —in raiding parties, in adventuring bands. They *could* have, but nobody knows for sure. Nobody knows what they looked like or what they wore (they *did* use buttons; these have been found in their graves). We can only be certain that around 2000 B.C., the Battle-ax People did appear south of the Caucasus. Two groups moved into Anatolia and another along the Zagros Mountains. We think their language was different from that spoken by the people of the hills.

Even today one does not hear Indo-European languages in the Caucasus Mountains (though Armenian, Kurdish, and Persian, just south, *are* Indo-European). The languages of the mountains are called simply Caucasic. Related to them is the language spoken by a tiny remnant group of people found far down the Zagros chain in northwest Pakistan.

We know that when the Battle-ax folk came they brought their horses along, because suddenly, around 1800 B.C., this new animal figures in writings of the Mesopotamian city folk as "the ass of foreign parts." Whether the horses arrived hitched to carts (which, in view of the terrain, seems unlikely) or whether they were ridden (no archaeological evidence of this) is not known.

There is one thing more. About this time in Luristan—that part of the Zagros chain just northeast of the middle Tigris—metalworkers among the hill folk began casting items for horses—rings for guiding reins along cart poles, ornaments for the harness. They also began to make ceremonial battle-axes, some of them cast in the form of horse's heads. Now these hill folk had long been skilled smiths. Their ancestors had pounded cold copper into pins at least five thousand years before the steppe nomads were to learn about copper at all, indeed before they were to come into existence as a people. It was from the hill folk that people of the Tigris and Euphrates river plain acquired the knowledge of metals that enabled them to smelt metal ores, to create new art styles and motifs for their growing cities. In time the hill folk simply settled into a cultural backwater, copying the styles of others. But when the Battle-ax People appeared, the metal smiths took fresh inspiration. Every useful metal article was adorned with fantastic animals, strange forms and shapes unlike anything to be seen among the city people of the plain.

Though some Battle-ax warriors no doubt went back over the

Mesopotamia

Caucasus after their years of adventuring, others stayed behind, married local girls, and made peace with the hillmen. And why not? Their battle skills and horsemanship must have given them considerable social standing. And there was one other inducement. The high, lush valleys of the hill country were perfect for the breeding of fine horses. So some men stayed behind. In time others joined them, perhaps bringing wives and cattle along. And the immigrants multiplied and with their hillmen followers became known to history as the Kassites.

Sometime around 1800 B.C. they began filtering onto the Tigris and Euphrates plain. Perhaps they had run out of new adventuring territory for their young men, or perhaps they had heard tales of the rich cities told by hillmen who had themselves raided there from time to time. However it came to pass, the new migration was on, and the Kassite warriors moved down from the hills to encounter the Kingdom of Babylonia. They now had light carts with spoked wheels. (No one knows whether the chariot was invented by Kassites or by their cousins farther north and east.) With their horses and weaponry they must have made attractive mercenary soldiers. During the next two hundred years they came into greater and greater prominence, until by 1550 B.C. or so they had somehow—by raids, by battles, by political maneuver—toppled the dynasty founded by King Hammurabi and taken power themselves.

Afterward, though they remained a sort of warrior caste apart from the rest of the population, the Kassites changed nothing about Babylonia. In fact, they tried to turn back the clock to older Babylonian days and ways. They learned to admire everything about their new realm—the clothes, the furniture, the customs. The once-loved bronzes of the hills—the fantastic animal figures, the axes so marvelously wrought—were not imported. No doubt they seemed crude and barbarous amid the sophisticated splendor of Babylon. The Kassites even dropped their own language and spoke and wrote in Akkadian, a Semitic language native to the region. At least, they used Akkadian for all official purposes. Because of this wholesale borrowing of Babylonian ways, we know little of the Kassites beyond their names, the names of their gods, and a few odd words and numbers compiled by some industrious scribe, no doubt for the purpose of ingratiating himself with the new masters. Both the names of Kassite gods and presumed representations of them found in the hills remind us of gods worshiped by the Battle-ax Aryans who went to India, and by their cousins, the Persians, who would later conquer Babylonia.

No, nothing changed in Babylonia when the Kassites came. They were themselves changed, changed to fit a pattern that was old long before brilliant Babylon had been built—a pattern as old as civilization itself. For it was in this land, down where the Tigris and Euphrates rivers run into the Persian Gulf, that civilized life, the life of cities, had had its first beginning. It was from here, from the land called Sumer, that city life had spread out west and north and even east, perhaps as far as China.

To catch a glimpse of these city beginnings, we must move backward in time, two thousand years backward, leaving the Kassites just as they are emerging onto the river plain, and picking up yet another, earlier group of new arrivals—the city-building Sumerians.

Just who the Sumerians were and where they came from nobody knows for sure. The language they spoke was surely different from those spoken by natives in the area: the desert nomads and the prosperous farmers among whom the newcomers settled. Words of these other, prior languages were incorporated into Sumerian, which was itself neither Indo-European nor Semitic nor even akin to any language now known.

Sumerians called themselves simply the Black-headed People. Some maintained they had come from a faraway city to the mountainous east, a city they called Aratta. Others claimed to have arrived by sea from a distant land. The fact that they built artificial high places (tree-planted "hills of heaven") on which to worship and pictured their gods standing on real hills suggests an original upland home. And yet, certain similarities with the early Indus civilization across the Persian Gulf, plus the situation of their oldest city, Eridu, right on what was then the shore line, makes the water route seem a possibility. Some scholars believe the Sumerians never "arrived" at all but were there in Mesopotamia all the time, growing and developing out of the old village settlements that had been there since the river marshes had been drained. Others think the Sumerians were simply the end result of several different waves of people, each of whom added to the general tradition.

However the Sumerians got to Mesopotamia, one thing is certain: they came to stay. Shortly after their appearance real temples rose where there had been only modest ceremonial centers. Around these temples true cities collected, walled and guarded cities all along the Euphrates and on canals leading into it. In the cities metalworkers were in demand, and businessmen and merchants rose to prominence. People took to using seal stones as marks of identification, and shortly thereafter (about 3500 B.C.) the first known picture writing appeared, incised on a square of soft limestone.

With the first writing came a host of other firsts: the first schools and the first schoolmasters; the first teaching assistants, the first home-work, "apple polishing," graduation, and all the rest. Sumerians were first to describe that product of the schoolroom, the learned fool, whom the Greeks would later call *sophosmoros.* It still persists in our own *sophomoric*—a word describing the conceited youth with some schooling but not yet enough to be truly wise.

Sumerians were the first devoted legalists, the first framers and re-corders of city laws—and not just laws but legal processes of every conceivable sort. Whether will or contract or family dispute—no matter was too small to escape the devoted attention of judge and scribe.

Today, when we do a page of arithmetic problems or tot up ex-penses or balance a budget, we do it in just ten number symbols (0–9). These are workable for any given quantity because they have place value. And they have place value because the Sumerians invented it.

The use of fractions began with the Sumerians. They had the first multiplication tables, the first tables of squares and square roots, cubes and cube roots. They were first to make tables to help compute the sizes of circles and the areas of fields and gardens. Western measurements of length, area, capacity, and weight still correspond roughly to the Sumerian originals.

Sumerian doctors wrote out the first prescriptions, which were based more on observation and experience and less on magic than were those of peoples who came along somewhat later in the game. Sumerian sculptors made the first likenesses of gods that were scaled to human form. Sumerians took to the rivers in boats with the world's first sails, and to the roads and trails in what might have been the world's first wheeled carts. Sumerian engineers made the first ambitious canals, dikes, weirs, and reservoirs, all to help drain the marshy land, the vast flats of mud from which were made the world's first bricks; mud which provided the world's first writing tablets. Sumerian tablet writing came to be ideographic—composed of stamped, cuneiform characters which could be (and were) used to record the many languages spoken by later people in Mesopotamia.

It was not only in practical matters that Sumerians chalked up "firsts." Many of the world's most cherished myths, stories, sayings, and proverbs (perhaps most of them) can be traced back to Sumerian originals. Part of this rich heritage came to us by way of Babylonia and its successive rulers, by way of Greece (whose people were always quick to pick up good ideas wherever they could be found), and by way of the Judeo-Christian Bible.

Perhaps as early as 2000 B.C. the Hebrews discovered Sumer (the land of Shinar, they called it). The Old Testament says that Abraham and his family came originally from the city of Ur. A thousand years later, Hebrews were taken back captive to Mesopotamia, where, through their Babylonian masters, they heard again the old Sumerian tales. Though they sternly resisted the gods and the ways of these city folk, they could not resist the tales, which eventually found their way even into the sacred books themselves. The story of the Tower of Babel, for example, very accurately describes the great Ziggurat of Ur, that great staged tower of brick which Abraham's people certainly beheld and which the Hebrew captives saw, too, in Babylonian reconstructions. Eden is like the fabled Dilmun of the Sumerians, a land where lion and lamb lie down together, and hunger and sickness are not. There was once a Sumerian Job who, like the Biblical Job, suffered undeservedly and wondered why. And the Ten Commandments, carved in stone and given by God, recall the many Mesopotamian law codes dictated from Above.

Most famous of all the Sumerian stories concerns a flood, a disastrous flood which all but wrecked creation, a flood in which only one good

man was saved along with his family and his animals. He was saved by divine warning and had the good sense to build a big boat. There really was such a flood in Mesopotamia before the Sumerian arrival, for the evidences of it have been uncovered by archaeologists. It did not wreck all creation, of course, but it did bring disaster to much of the land between the rivers, which was indeed all creation to the people who lived there at the time, and the terrible memory of it lived on in the legends of later times.

Ziusudra was the pure and blameless hero-king of the Sumerian flood story. Babylonian scribes later rewrote it to include a lengthy description of the ark and the scene in which birds are sent out to find land. They also gave the hero another name. Ut-napishtim, they called him. When the Hebrews recounted the story, they called their hero Noah. It was a story of irresistible appeal in those days, making its way into nearly every ancient literature. The Egyptians translated the cuneiform version into hieroglyphs. Even the floodless Greeks adopted it as the tale of Deucalion.

It is a story that appeals to us still. Every few years somebody writes a new version of the flood. It has turned up in several popular modern plays and stories without number. Writers today, however, are more inclined to substitute for the watery disaster an up-to-the-minute atomic one, and underground shelters and spaceships in flight have replaced the old familiar ark. The new Ararat is no longer on earth but far away on another planet. The problem remains the same. What to save and what to leave behind? How to start humanity afresh and make it a better humanity, with all its weaknesses purged away and all its virtues reaffirmed? How to keep the good things of civilization while discarding the bad? And who is to decide which is which? These were questions asked first by the Sumerians.

No doubt about it. The Sumerians were inventive people, breaking trails all people after them would follow. But like the Greeks of later times, they could not see themselves aright—being at once greater and smaller than their own estimation. Always they are pictured as pleasant, smiling chaps, unfailingly calm and kind. The fact is, they were a quarrelsome lot among themselves. City fought city over farm land and water rights and slaves and the superior merits of their various city gods. Their chief priests were supplanted in time by war leaders who took over many priestly duties. A leader always called himself *ensi,* the steward, the tenant farmer of the city god, elected by him and responsible to him (or her) for the city's proper management. Though the god (and his city) could be made the vassal of a stronger god (and *his* city), no god could be deprived of his abode. The city was the indivisible social unit.

Some ensis grew rich and powerful. Some seem to have been deified. Perhaps they were royal sacrifices. In any case, some went into their graves with their wives and all their retinues for company. A-ani-pad-a and his queen, Shub-ad, were given just such a burial party in the royal cemetery at Ur.

Though there was constant rivalry among the Sumerian cities, there was a vague sense of identity, too. Enough for them to call themselves by one name and to recognize one city as sacred to the lot. That was holy Nippur with its temple to Enlil, breath of the air, chief among gods. By 2500 B.C. the cities were vying for the active leadership of all, and one after another seized control.

In the midst of all the strife, however (or perhaps because of it), the Sumerian civic sense was being sharpened and developed. Remarkably sane laws were devised and civil rights were guaranteed—even for women and slaves, both of whom were allowed to own property, manage it, appeal in court, and move about nearly at will. Capital punishment was meted out much less frequently than it would be later in Assyrian times. Fines were often levied instead.

The earliest Sumerian law code yet discovered dates from 2100 B.C.

or thereabouts and bears the name of Ur-Nammu. But there were certainly codes which preceded it. There must have been, because Urukagina, King of Lagash (*c.* 2400 B.C.), criticized the old laws and tried to reform them. He describes just how he went about this in a clay document which has come down to us. So bent was he, however, on wiping out graft and corruption, so sure was he of being divinely rewarded, divinely protected for his goodness that he failed to keep his army up to snuff. Lagash was defeated by the city of Umma (the two cities had been at odds for a long time), and Urukagina was summarily ousted. It is comforting to learn that his ruthless conqueror was also removed when the mighty Sargon came to power.

Sargon was a desert chieftain who had taken up service with the king of Kish, a Semitic city near Babylon, and settled down to absorb Sumerian culture. He learned his lessons well. Having gathered an army, he set out to annex Sumer and did just that. At last, sometime around 2370 B.C., the quarreling cities were united in an enforced peace and a larger political union. Sargon carried on the old traditions, but he insisted that his own Semitic language (henceforth called Akkadian, after Agade, his capital) be spoken as well as the Sumerian tongue. And he garrisoned the Sumerian cities with his own troops, led by his own kinfolk. For the first time, Sumerian civilization began to spread northward with the Akkadian armies. Old records suggest that Sargon marched all the way to the Mediterranean, marched east to encircle kindred Assyria, a group of small cities built by Semitic people midway up the Tigris River. He then moved north into Anatolia.

This precocious empire could not last, and it did not. Mountaineers from the Zagros—Gutians, "stinging serpents of the hills," Sumerians would later call them—moved in to take over, and though Sargon's descendants fought hard and well against them, his empire was overcome. Assyria was now independent, and so were the cities of Sumer. Rejoicing, the Sumerians said Enlil had called down the Gutians to punish Sargonid rulers for the destruction of holy Nippur. And they coexisted pleasantly with the Gutians, while Gudea, Ensi of Lagash, sparked a modest Sumerian revival. He was apparently a patron of the arts—at least when he was the subject. More statues of Gudea have been found than of any other Sumerian dignitary.

Around 2150 B.C., Ur waxed strong enough to throw the Gutians out and form a new, a federated, a truly Sumerian empire, which extended far up the upper Tigris. This was the time of Ur-Nammu and the rebuilding of the great Ziggurat. We call it the Third Dynasty of Ur.

All the while, hungry desert men speaking yet another Semitic language, the Amurru (or Amorites), threatened Sumer's western flank. They, along with Elamites from the east, eventually broke the power of Ur. Sumer was dead now as a political entity. Kings of Sumerian cities bore Semitic names and spoke Akkadian, though the old Sumerian language was still used in religious life much the way Latin has long been the ceremonial language of the Catholic Church. But the old ways were undergoing transformation, being reshaped to the uses of the new peoples who were absorbing them.

Desert Amorites annexed the last of the old Sumerian holdouts. Hammurabi, the sixth king of the Amorite line, founded a new empire with its capital in Babylon, an ancient city where Sumerians and Akkadians had long lived together peaceably, dreading only incursions of "the Westerners"—the desert Amorites. Now descendants of those same Amorites made Babylon the most brilliant city of the ancient world.

The Land Between the Rivers became known as Babylonia, and everyone began to forget about the little string of Sumerian cities down by the gulf which had brought it all into being. The great Hammurabi was thought for a long time to be the world's first lawgiver. We know now his laws were built on Sumerian models, changed somewhat to suit the temper of the new rulers who enforced them and the new people governed by them. They were harsher laws, on the whole, than the Sumerian models. They demanded "an eye for an eye, and a tooth for a tooth." Women were no longer so free as before, slaves had fewer rights, and punishment was geared to fit both rank and crime.

The old gods remained in their heavens, but the goddesses suffered the same eclipse as did living women down below. You would never have known that, once upon a time, the land had put much of its faith in a great earth mother. And a new and powerful god, Marduk of Babylon, pushed aside even Father Enlil to take leadership of the pantheon.

It was at this point (about 1600 B.C.) that the Kassites arrived in Babylonia and they ruled it for four hundred years—longer than any dynasty had done before. Babylonia was not first among powers during the Kassite reign. No great buildings were erected, no great battles won, no innovations made in law or art or religion. But the tradition, the heritage of the past, was preserved and nurtured whether the Kassites understood its origins or no.

Sometime around 1200, Assyria, up north, gathered strength and successfully challenged the Kassites. The remnants that survived the attack fled back to the Zagros, to the dimly remembered homelands. And Assyria became a great military power, the mightiest and most ruthless the world had yet seen. Her kings, her soldiers were nothing at all like the smiling Gudea, nothing like Sumerian spearmen, nodding pleasantly in their leather helmets, and there was about them not the slightest hint of the Kassite strain of fantasy. They were instead portly and muscular and a little cruel, and they liked their statuary to show these things about them. But they were antiquarians, too, oddly enough. Assurbanipal, an Assyrian monarch who could calmly level a dozen cities and carry their inhabitants off to captivity, kept a marvelous library in which many old tablets from ancient times were preserved. The tablets in his library have given us much that we know now of Sumer in its palmiest days.

Even the last echo of the Kassite interlude appears in the writings of an Assyrian monarch, who complained bitterly about the troublesome barbarians of the hills. It seems that a certain Kashtaritu, king of the old Kassite stronghold, was trying to unite new, incoming Battle-ax warriors—the Cimmerians and the Medes—against Assyria. Whether the Kassite king was punished for his ambition or whether he was successful is not recorded. In any case, Assyria's days were numbered. After 612 B.C., Babylonia fell first to the Medes, then to the Persians, who united it with the eastern hills and the steppe beyond to form a new and still greater empire. Indeed, it was nearly a world state, into which old Sumerian traditions and new ideas were now poured, a world state which would itself one day decline and die.

The whole history of Mesopotamia is, in fact, a seesaw tale of conquest and regeneration and conquest all over again—of pendulum swings between people of the desert and people of the hills and steppes, between languages, and much later, between religions. But the essential tradition has never wavered. Always the good seeds have been preserved (as Ziusudra survived the flood) to blossom again in new and better gardens.

2. Hittites

Governing in Anatolia

Turning west as they crossed the Caucasus, the Battle-ax People we know as the Hittites made their way into Anatolia, the land that is now modern Turkey. Something more than a peninsula, something less than a continent, the Anatolian land mass links east and west and divides the Black Sea from the Mediterranean. From its rocky Asiatic roots pour the Tigris and Euphrates rivers to mark the beginning of Mesopotamia; its western shores all but touch Europe. Anatolia is a bridge, a hilly highway, over which many feet have passed and on which many a traveler has settled down to stay. In Anatolia's southern region there can be seen today the remains of Old Stone Age hunters, Middle Stone Age gatherers, and earliest Neolithic farmers. Here old life ways shifted and merged and changed.

Far from hovering on the bare fringes of developing civilization, Anatolia seems always to have been in the very thick of things. There were farms here and villages and even good-sized towns long before farming moved down into the lush river valley of Mesopotamia. It was from Anatolia that farming, house types, and nobody knows how many less tangible notions traveled across the Hellespont and into Europe. It was in Anatolia that the first pottery of the Middle East was made. And though writing, it is true, was invented elsewhere, though true cities had their beginning elsewhere, there was something in Anatolia that helped provide the riches, the leisure, the intensive trade that made these new developments possible. Anatolia had metals.

Both Mesopotamia and Syria are bare of metal ore, but the people of Anatolia and the Zagros Mountains have known metals since about 8000 B.C., when they began beating cold copper into pins and blades and other useful items. It was probably somewhere in eastern Anatolia that the knowledge of copper smelting was discovered (around 6000 B.C. perhaps?). And it was from this area that both technical knowledge and the ores themselves were carried abroad. The similarities of casting techniques seen in copper objects found in Sumerian Ur and those found at town sites in central and west Anatolia tell us how widespread metal trade was in the early Middle East.

One trading center was the ancient town which now lies buried under a mound of Turkish soil and is called Catal Hüyük—the little hill, or mound, of Catal. For its time (6500–5600 B.C.) it was perhaps the richest town in the Neolithic world. Certainly it was the largest. A spread of thirty-two acres is no size to be sneezed at, especially when you consider that its most important rival, Jericho in Palestine, bound only ten acres within its walls.

Catal Hüyük was a town of businessmen and superb craftsmen. From imported flint, obsidian, and sea shells; from a native abundance

CAUCASUS MTS.

BLACK SEA

PALA
Alaca Hüyük
● Hattusas

espont
● Troy

TAURUS MTS.

LUWIANS
(LUKKA-LANDS)
KONYA PLAIN
Çatal Hüyük

MITANNI

ZAGROS MTS.

Euphrates R.

Tigris R.

CYPRUS

MEDITERRANEAN

● Kadesh

The Hittite Empire

of copper and ornamental stones, its workers manufactured jewelry and all sorts of useful and luxury items in great demand abroad. But there are revelations quite beyond the economic facts of life. The people of Çatal Hüyük were deeply religious. In their rabbit-warren town, built one dwelling next to another and each one entered by way of ladders and a door in the roof (think of a Hopi pueblo in the American Southwest), there were hidden dozens of sacred rooms, churches really. These places of worship were adorned with bewildering varieties of paintings, statues, and reliefs. Most represented the chief deity of the town—a goddess sometimes shown as a young girl, sometimes as a mother, sometimes as a crone. Often she was painted standing on a leopard's back and accompanied by a young god, spouse, or son. Sometimes another god was shown as well—a bearded, older god standing on a bull. Often he was merely represented by bull's or ram's horns. Smaller symbols—human hands, crosses, tiny horns, birds of prey—decorated walls everywhere. In these motifs, in the figures of goddess and gods, we can see the beginnings of a religious pattern so vital, so meaningful, that it was to dominate the thinking of all who came to Anatolia and settled there and of many people beyond Anatolia's shores. This includes the Battle-ax people.

They came early to Anatolia. Migrants from the Caucasus who arrived sometime around 2000 B.C. encountered not only the small city-kingdoms of the native folk but several tribes of their own cousins, who had perhaps swung around the Black Sea and over the Hellespont several hundred years before. The record of these early intruders can be read in the destruction they left behind. Troy—that ill-fated city—suffered at their hands the worst burning in its long career of successive disasters. All around the southern shores of the peninsula and up into the Konya Plain, towns were burned, leveled, their farms and dwellings trodden under, grazed over by herd animals of the incoming nomads. Most, the archaeological record tells us, were not rebuilt.

And yet it was not long before these marauding nomads were at least partly tempered to the Anatolian pattern, bent to civilized ways. Slowly they spread out and settled in. One group acquired a set of hieroglyphs in which its language could be written. This seems to have been the Indo-European language we know as Luwian, or something very close to it. Luwian settlements and those of their near kin clustered around the southern and eastern shore lines. Other groups of Battle-ax invaders, such as the Pala, occupied parts of the north. Around 2200 B.C. Luwian names begin to turn up in the documents of other peoples in the Middle East.

Dating from this time, too, is an interesting site in north central Anatolia. It was once part of a rich city, perhaps a tiny kingdom.

People lived there and worked there and laughed and loved. Now it is known by its "mound" name—Alaca Hüyük—and it is of interest to us chiefly because of its cemetery. The graves are royal, beyond a doubt, and exceedingly rich in treasure—objects of bronze, silver, gold, even iron. More interesting still is the architecture of the graves themselves. They are stone-lined and timber-roofed, each a sort of mortuary house. In each were found the heads and hoofs of cattle and rams, occasionally the bodies of dogs. Each housed one or perhaps two persons (husband and wife). The royal corpses were provided with weapons—knives and spears and battle-axes and "standards" on which were mounted stags, bulls, and sun symbols—all the usual furnishings to be found in the graves of nomad chieftains beyond the Caucasus. Does this simply reflect the fashion of the time? Or had the royal family of Alaca Hüyük connections with Battle-ax People—the Luwians of the south, perhaps? Were they themselves Battle-ax folk? No one knows. But the resemblances remain, and also the fact that Alaca Hüyük lies in the area that Battle-ax Hittites were later to make their home and from which they would dominate all the motley, polyglot folk of great Anatolia.

They did not call themselves Hittites at first. Their ancient name seems to have been something like Nesite. After they appropriated the little kingdom and the people of Hatti, however, they adopted the old name for themselves—much the way the new proprietor of a shop keeps his predecessor's name over the door so as not to offend old customers.

Hittites first turn up in written records about 1900 B.C. Assyrian traders based in Anatolia wrote back to the home office about the new people, mentioning a name here and a name there. A little later the Hittites themselves learned cuneiform writing—not the style used by Assyrians, but an old-fashioned Babylonian script, of just the sort likely to have been treasured by provincial scribes far from the great centers of Mesopotamian academic life. Now Hittites could keep their own records. Since cuneiform writing was by now simply a set of all-purpose syllable signs, it could be used for a variety of languages, and the Hittites did just that. They never gave up their own language—as the Kassites down Zagros way seem to have done after invading Babylonia—but they could be accomplished linguists whenever it suited their purpose. Even ancient Hatti was retained for religious services, though much translating and interpretation was necessary to make the sonorous phrases intelligible to the average communicant. The content of those services remained very much in the old Anatolian pattern, which the Hittites enthusiastically adopted, possibly because they found many of its elements congenial and familiar. Their old thunder god of the steppes, for example, merged easily with the bearded Anatolian weather god. To the religious art of Hatti they added only a few motifs: a few of the old, loved animal figures and a battle-ax or two.

All in all, there is little about the early Hittites to set them apart from any other group of invading barbarians who picked up civilized ways and soon became lost in the native population. As the Hittite state grew and developed, however, a certain individuality began to be plain, a certain style in political matters that was somehow different from that of other Middle Eastern states.

Whatever else they came to be, the Hittites were first of all and always good soldiers. Not stylish ones, perhaps. Their three-man chariots were heavy, and they had to import teachers of horsemanship from nearby Mitanni. In the strategy of their king-generals, however, in the discipline of their troops, in the quality of their military engineering, the Hittites were unmatched.

They first felt strong enough to challenge the local kings around

1800 B.C., when a half-legendary leader called Anittas took the city that Hittites were later to make their capital—Hattusas. A century and a half later, the great Labarnas (whose name would come to mean "king" in Hatti as *Caesar* would mean "king" in Rome) "made the seas his frontiers." When Labarnas was king (so a later chronicle tells us), "his sons, his brothers, his connections by marriage, and his blood relations were united," and though the Hittites were a small people, their unity was their invincible strength. But already during the time of Labarnas's successor, Hattusilis I, the relatives were plotting treachery. The heir presumptive, a nephew, had to be passed over and an adoptive son named as heir. To legalize this act, the king called together the "assembly—fighting men and dignitaries," explained his reasons, and asked for their consent. For the king was, after all, merely a warrior among warriors—after the manner of nomad raiders—and needed their support.

When the adopted son, the new heir, came to power, the wide territories taken by Hittites proved indigestible, the long-threatened palace revolt broke out, and the kingdom collapsed in disorder for fifty years. At last, in 1525 B.C., a new king maneuvered his way to the throne. This king meant to stay, and he meant his legal heirs to succeed him. Most of all, he meant to make the kingdom secure in its land and in its organization. Toward these ends, he drew up a set of rules governing the succession and setting bounds on the behavior of king and nobles alike. To make the rules seem reasonable, he outlined a history of all that had happened among the Hittites up to that moment. It is the earliest such writing known to us. It also accomplished its purpose. Never again would the Hittite succession be seriously in doubt. This king, one Telepinus by name, also achieved another first, a diplomatic treaty with a neighboring and vassal state. After Telepinus, the fever for planning grew so intense that Hittite

kings regularly saw to it that laws throughout the kingdom were compiled and periodically examined, that military annals were written and records kept.

Sometime around 1500 B.C. the Hittites developed a new and better way of smelting iron. The old methods had yielded a metal really no better than bronze, but now the Hittites began to produce something harder and more durable. Cannily, they kept the smelting secret to themselves and sent only small samples of the "good iron" to royal neighbors.

The leading powers of the fifteenth-century world were Egypt, Kassite Babylonia, and the Kingdom of Mitanni, a state touching Hittite lands, a state, like Hatti, ruled by a Battle-ax nobility. Hittite lands were by now extensive, for the rulers had managed to bind in alliance to themselves most of the other Anatolian states. Their neighbors and rivals, the Mitannians, were forever trying to wean away or to annex their southern provinces, forever bribing the wild tribesmen of the hills to revolt. Hittite kings (or, to be more accurate, emperors) bided their time until they could deal with the Mitannian menace once and for all. Finally the moment came, a time when Mitanni's Egyptian allies were occupied with their own problems. A lightning Hittite raid on the Mitannian capital, a shuffling of rulers there, and suddenly —sometime around 1370 B.C.—the old balance of power was realigned. Hatti was one of the Big Three, and Mitanni was not. The sudden rise to eminence had its price. The Hittites found themselves standing toe to toe with mighty Egypt.

The inevitable showdown came at an oasis in the desert east of the Euphrates, at the Battle of Kadesh in 1286 B.C. For a very long time this campaign was known to modern scholars only through the boastful accounts of the Egyptian Pharaoh, who claimed to have won the battle. A Hittite version of it has never been found. It is worth noting, however, that after the battle the Pharaoh came quickly to terms with the Hittite king and withdrew his claims to influence in the northern part of Syria—not quite the reactions of a conqueror. A few years and a new set of monarchs later, Egyptians and Hittites were on the most friendly footing imaginable—exchanging correspondence and marrying one another's sisters and daughters, calling one another "brother." Politics, it is said, makes strange bedfellows. The new-found amity was rooted in concern, for Assyria, having regained its independence from Mitanni, was fast becoming mighty in the east.

And yet Assyria was not to bring down the Hittite Empire. From 1240 B.C. on a new wave of Battle-ax raiders surged around the Black Sea and over the Hellespont. Some of the vassal states—rebellious as always—joined them. Eventually an Indo-European people called the Phrygians engulfed great Hatti. Related raiders called the Sea People in Egyptian records took to boats, gave Egypt a hard fight, and then peeled off into Libya. One group settled in southern Syria. They were the tribal Philistines, and from this name came the land name, Palestine.

Hittite refugees converged on the southeastern domains, organized into little kingdoms, and retained for another five hundred years a certain glowing image until Assyria swallowed all. It was from the writings and art of the new Hittite kingdoms that modern scholars learned there had once been an old Hittite empire. The new sparked a search for the old, for Hattusas and the clay tablets hopefully deposited there.

And how do the Hittites seem to us as they march out of their clay tablets, their statues, and their vast stone reliefs? Certainly they must not be accounted an especially inventive or brilliant people. Their art is bulky without being powerful, pleasant without being memorable, and in some ways almost crude. Its themes and styles have been borrowed wholesale from more imaginative neighbors. Their literature is limited and without pretension. Hittites did not write poetry as the Egyptians did, nor epics in the Babylonian manner. Even their religious forms were not their own.

All in all they seem to us as practical, as self-possessed as the Romans would be in later times and climes, and a good deal more modest. Like the Romans, the Hittites could fight. Like the Romans, they could also rule.

Perhaps this was so because Anatolia was never of a piece—one people, one language. Perhaps it was also because the Hittites themselves were so outnumbered that they had to learn diplomacy, tolerance, and (in a relative sense) real mildness in order to hold their empire together. And yet, unlike the Kassites, they were not fated to be overwhelmed by older cultures too brilliant to be withstood. The little Anatolian kingdoms were no Babylons—not even minor-league ones. For all their borrowings, Hittites kept their identity and in time came to be rather different from their neighbors. The domain they ruled was different, too.

In the first place, it was really a sort of federation. Small local states kept their individuality and their own laws. They were bound to Hattusas by treaties which spelled out the rights and obligations that obtained between them and the central government. The Hittites did not take hostages to guarantee the good behavior of their vassals. They did not inflict cruel punishments when vassals revolted (and a few did so regularly). There were no flayings or impalings of captured enemies in the later Assyrian manner.

Hittite law codes—those of the central government—were constantly being revised toward more lenient interpretations and milder punishment. In any case, the emphasis was more on setting things right, more on requiting an injured party, making good his loss, than on achieving absolute justice of the "eye for an eye, tooth for a tooth" sort. Slaves had civil rights, and women enjoyed as high a position as ever they had done in ancient Sumer. Even so, the decrees of the central government were always subject to local interpretation. Circuit judges and garrison commanders were forever being admonished by the king to respect local customs and local laws.

Perhaps it was not so much piety as political astuteness that sent the king every winter on visits to all the major cult centers of the empire. Eventually these religious duties took precedence over all else as he tried to please all the people all the time. For the Hittite king was considered neither a god's representative nor a god as were the kings of other countries around and about. He had begun his royal career as a military leader, first among equals, and something of that role remained throughout all of Hittite history.

Hittite kings felt the need to seek the advice of assemblies and to explain their actions and the tenor of preceding events. Though they may have lacked verse, they did write history with an attempt at objectivity unusual in those times. About their own doings the kings commented with modesty and sometimes with painful self-revelation. The old Hattusilis whose nephew betrayed him said:

> I, the king, called him my son, embraced him, exalted him, and cared for him continually. But he showed himself a youth not fit to be seen; he shed no tears, he showed no pity, he was cold and heartless. . . . The word of the king he has not laid to heart, but the word of his mother, the serpent, he has laid to heart. . . . Enough! He is my son no more. . . . Behold, I have given my son Labarna a house! I have given him arable land in plenty, sheep in plenty I have given him. Let him now eat and drink. So long as he is good he may come up to the city. . . . Behold, Mursili is now my son.

And then to his newly adopted son, really his grandson, he added,

Till now no one of my family has obeyed my will; but thou, my son Mursili, thou must obey it. . . . Thou shalt remember my words of wisdom in your heart. With my fighting men and my nobles thou shalt deal leniently. If one of them commits a wrong, either before a god or by uttering blasphemous words, then consult the *pankus* [the assembly of nobles]. Any dispute shall be referred to the pankus.

And finally,

Thou shalt wash my dead body according to the custom. Hold me to your heart, and holding me to your heart, lay me in the earth.

A later monarch was troubled by a domineering stepmother, a Kassite princess, who he claimed had killed his beloved wife and caused him to have a speech impediment (through witchcraft, perhaps?). To the gods he prayed,

Because I appear before you as your priest and servant, be kindly disposed toward me. Drive out the pain from my heart, and from my soul lift fear.

Between the Phrygians and the Assyrians, all the Hittites' patient work came tumbling down and was in time forgotten. Almost, but not quite. Hittite political wisdom and tolerance were to have a certain effect on the later Persians and on another people as well. Always there had been close ties between Anatolia and mainland Greece. Some early Greeks seem to have felt they had two homes, one of which was across the Hellespont. Perhaps it is not too farfetched to suppose that what later came to flower in classical Greece and eventually in Rome— the governing forms, the appreciation of objectivity, the emphasis on history—owed something to a dim and distant beginning in Anatolia.

3. Mitanni

A Kingdom of Charioteers

Times around the year 2000 B.C. were very troubled in much of the Middle East. It was not the Battle-ax People alone who were responsible. From highlands somewhere near Lake Van in what we now call Armenia came clever mountaineers who slowly filtered down into the cities of the plain. And from out of Arabia came marauding desert men, as fierce in war and far more single-minded in peace than ever the Battle-ax folk were to be. All three groups converged on the coastal arc of what is now Syro-Palestine.

What they found was a land of small cities. Those on the coast, such as Byblos and Ugarit, were turned outward to the sea, poised to attract any maritime trade that came their way. Those back in the hills, perched above the fertile Jordanian valley or in the Lebanon, were

turned in on themselves and ringed with high walls. They were royal seats of various petty princes ruling over tiny farm domains. Presumably the walled cities functioned in much the same way as did the wooden stockades of the American West, which provided sanctuary for farmers when Indian raids threatened. Raiders in the Jordanian valley and points north seem to have been nomads, fierce shepherds from the desert behind the hills. This seesaw contest between desert and settled folk—if such it was—had already had a long history. Jericho, the first of the Jordanian walled towns, was built about 8000 B.C., almost before its people had entirely taken to the farming way of life and while they were still very largely dependent on hunting and gathering for their food. Even in those early days, however, they had amassed wealth enough to need the protection of walls. For Jericho was doubly blessed: it had an inexhaustible spring and it was on the crossroads of ancient travel. No doubt it was caravan traffic that made Jericho's people rich.

Raiders into the sown lands of Syro-Palestine encountered no speech barrier. Both the coastal area and its Arabian backdrop seem to have been home for time out of mind to peoples speaking Semitic languages. This fact is amply borne out in the catalogue of place names to be heard there still. For some reason, place names seldom change. Whatever a mountain or river is first called is apt to be the name it keeps for good, no matter how many different people come to live in the vicinity. (Think of all the American rivers and mountains with Indian or Spanish names—Mississippi, Connecticut, Appalachian, Sierra Madre.) The oldest place names in Palestine are (as archaeologist W. F. Albright tells us) archaic Semitic in origin—Labnon (Lebanon), Jordan, Jabbok. Early towns often took the names of shrines around which their populations had collected (all the "beth" names, such as Bethlehem or Bethel—*beth* meaning "house"—belong in this group), and the names stuck however many times the original settlement was rebuilt. With desert folk around 2000 B.C. came tribal names to be affixed to certain localities, and the later Hebrews brought clan and family names. In the last few centuries, Arabic names have been added to the list. And in the last few decades have come the names in modern Hebrew.

Similarity of language has never been a guarantee of brotherly affection, however, and the desert tribes seem always to have been as eager to sack the towns of their richer fellows as those of strangers. City folk around the desert's fringe knew the nomads well but knew them by different names. Martu, the Sumerians called them, "people who know not grain." Early Babylonians (as we have seen) called them Amurru ("Westerners"). In early times the Egyptians used a name which translates as "sand ramblers." Later they picked up another to describe nomads beyond the Jordan. This was *'Apiru,* a word closely related to the familiar *Hebrew*. What the people of ancient Jericho called the desert raiders we do not know, for they had no means of writing the name.

In the period around 2000 B.C. the sporadic raids from the desert grew to a flood. This was the time that increasing forays by the Amorites were troubling Mesopotamia. In Syro-Palestine hundreds of towns were sacked and sheep sent to graze over the remains. Altogether it was the biggest disaster the desert men had yet wreaked in the area. Perhaps increasing dryness in their desert home had something to do with their depredations in richer lands. We only know they did come—wave after wave of them.

What they were like—these desert men—we can learn by consulting the first books of the Old Testament. For it is in this context of folk movement and unrest, the toppling of old kingdoms and the setting up of new ones, that the story of Abraham must be read. Sternly patriachal, family-centered, family-bound, the desert men tended to view their gods as family men, too—spiritual extensions of the clan father, the tribal sheik. Each god fought for his chosen people and punished them, too, when they failed in proper obedience. And they fought for him, thinking to bring him glory in the destruction of other gods and *their* chosen people. Many of these Semitic gods bore similar names—variations of El or Il or Elyon—which suggests a common origin in the dim past. The Syrian Ba'al, the Mesopotamian ilu (gods), Allah of Islam, and Elohim of the Old Testament all reflect their desert beginnings. It was to be the god of Abraham and Abraham's people, the wandering Hebrews, who would determine the shape of ethics in the Western world and give rise to two great world religions of later times—Christianity and Islam.

Powerful and original document that it is, the Bible yet reveals a debt to people encountered and new ideas assimilated along the Hebrew line of march. Some of these ideas were, as we have seen, borrowed from Sumerian sources. Other ideas were picked up in Palestine. It has long been thought that some aspects of the Bible are somehow out of the Hebrew character. Esau's selling his birthright for a "mess of pottage" has jarred many a Biblical scholar. Untypical, they thought. Not so odd, however, when the custom is connected with another people among whom it was common practice and who were well known to the Hebrews, who called them Horites. We know these people as the Hurrians.

The Hurrian mountaineers were moving out of the hills around Lake Van and down into northern Mesopotamia and Syro-Palestine at about the same time as the Amorites. Nobody knows much about them except that their language was different from both Indo-European and Semitic tongues. In the way the words were put together, it vaguely resembled old Sumerian and modern Turkish, but it was neither one nor the other. Perhaps it may yet prove to be akin to Gutian (spoken by the hillmen who invaded Sumer-Akkad) or to one of the other languages of the Caucasus and Zagros ranges. If Hurrian origins are mysterious, so is Hurrian influence—the full extent of which scholars are only just beginning to realize. Hurrian ideas, art motifs, and god names have turned up in Hittite country and down into Mesopotamia as well as into northern Syria. They seem to have settled in peacefully among the mercantile coastal towns and the tiny city kingdoms.

The Mitanni in the Middle East

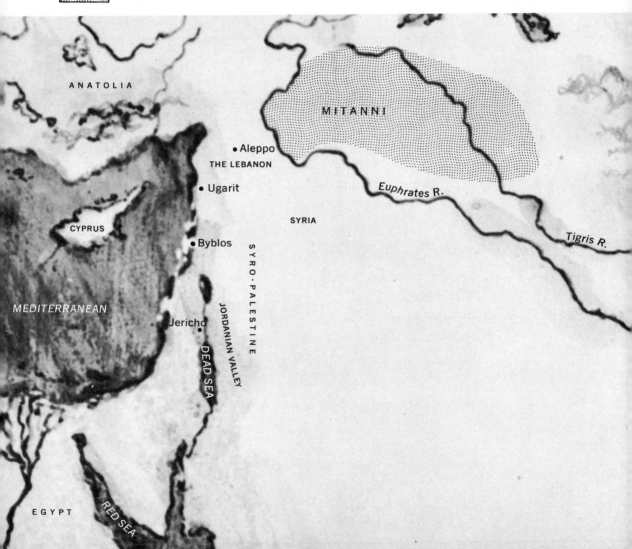

Sometimes—particularly in the area between the upper Tigris and Euphrates—they built towns for themselves. Most often they became incorporated into existing city structures, often occupying civil and religious positions of importance. They were seldom rulers, however. Their names do not appear in the diplomatic correspondence files uncovered in Egypt; the names of chiefs and rulers in Syro-Palestine were Semitic or Indo-European in origin. Hurrians and Battle-ax folk seem to have had a strange affinity: where one went, the other shortly followed, and there is no way of knowing which one arrived first.

The earliest hint of a Battle-ax presence in Syro-Palestine has been found in Byblos on a small limestone obelisk dated at about 2100 B.C. The obelisk was dedicated to the local prince by one Kukun, Lukka-Man. Were there then Luwians in Byblos—tamed, refined to the point of making diplomatic gifts? It would certainly seem so. Actually there was precious little use of writing in the Syro-Palestinian area between 2000 and 1500 B.C. What mentions there are of this part of the world must be sought in Mesopotamian and Egyptian writings. In one of these a Palestinian princeling is linked as coruler with one whose name is not Semitic but possibly Indo-European in origin. Clearly some change was taking place. But what?

We do know that around 1750 B.C. an army of invaders called the Hyksos moved through Syro-Palestine and into Egypt, toppling that ancient kingdom and installing their own Pharaoh. The army seems to have been led by Battle-ax People, chariot warriors called Maryannu. The name is Indo-European in origin, akin to the ancient Sanskrit *maryas,* which meant first "youth" and later "noble warrior," just as the Teutonic *knight* originally meant "youth." The word *maryannu* was later incorporated into Egyptian with the meaning "chariot warrior," but it was never used extensively until long after the invaders had been at last expelled from Egyptian soil. These invaders—foot soldiers and Maryannu alike—moved in waves through the coastal route to Egypt. Their graves, their forts, their buried weapons tell us so. But of their initial arrival in Syro-Palestine and their passage into Egypt there is nothing in writing—nothing in cuneiform, nothing in hieroglyphs. Nothing until the Hyksos had at last conquered and settled in.

During this period of historical silence but great turbulence a new kind of writing was invented. Somewhere in the Syro-Palestinian area an unknown genius invented the alphabet. The notion of using single sound signs instead of the idea signs or the syllable signs so popular for diplomatic correspondence throughout the civilized world seems to have been "in the air" around this time. Both the Mesopotamians and the Egyptians knew *how* to use single sound signs, but they could not see the possibilities of an alphabet. It remained to others, less wedded to an old way of writing, to seize the opportunity. Several experimental alphabets have been discovered in Palestine. One, unearthed in Ugarit, was based on cuneiform symbols. Another, based on Egyptian hieroglyphs, was found in Byblos, long one of Egypt's partners in commerce. The oldest of these sound-sign writings has been found in the Sinai Peninsula. It was in Sinai that the Egyptians had their copper and turquoise mines and there they employed men from Palestine and men from the desert. Whether the alphabet used there was brought to Sinai or invented on the spot, two things are clear: It was invented for the purpose of writing a Semitic language in signs borrowed from Egyptian hieroglyphs, and all present-day alphabets derive from it.

When turbulence in Syro-Palestine subsided, when records became more plentiful, tentative alphabetic writing was beginning to catch on —not among the ruling classes, to be sure, but among the common folk. Other changes were also visible. The old merchant leaders of towns had been replaced by Maryannu who had Indo-European names such as Indraruta, Bnon, Khyan, and Og, and who worshiped Indo-

European gods. The Battle-ax People were everywhere. Nowhere were they stronger than in Hurrian lands between the Tigris and Euphrates, a land known as the Kingdom of Mitanni, with its capital, Wassuggani, somewhere on the northern Habur River.

About 1550 B.C., when the motley army of Battle-ax Maryannu and their Palestinian allies were driven out of Egypt, they slowly fell back into the Mitannian homeland they had carved out for themselves beyond the Euphrates. Presumably Maryannu leaders and defenders in the cities of southern Palestine were also swept before the Egyptian armies. Eventually the little Palestinian cities of coast and hills found themselves alone to face the wrath of an Egypt determined to punish and put down the upstarts of this miserable coastal corridor. The cities were little, yes, but miserable, no. There were riches undreamed of in these cities whose merchants dressed opulently and whose rulers drove chariots copied from Maryannu models and made of gold. The little cities had for so long been tuned each to its own affairs, obediently bending whichever way the winds of world power blew—whether from mighty Egypt or mighty Babylonia—that they had never developed any sort of national identity, except briefly, while the Battle-ax Maryannu had been in charge.

Now, however, they scrabbled together—a royal guard from this town, a small army from that, nomad mercenaries from beyond the hills, and whatever Maryannu leaders were left to fight. The Egyptian Pharaoh, Thutmose I, overcame them easily. They accepted Egyptian vassaldom. What else could they do?

After that first Thutmose, however, there came a breathing space, and in that time (perhaps around 1500 B.C.), the Mitannian kings grew strong and began to woo the little states of Syro-Palestine, which were united, at least, in a common hatred of Egypt. And the winds of power again began to shift and blow from Mitanni-way. Assyria was incorporated into the Mitannian state, and even the Hittites began to feel the pressure of growing Mitannian might.

The Maryannu of Mitanni were few, their subjects were many, and so (like their Hittite cousins and rivals) they took care not to offend local custom. They wrote in the Hurrian language, but they never used Hurrian names or adopted Hurrian gods. Their own deities—Indra, Mitra, Varuna—appear in Mitannian treaties as guarantors of Mitannian good faith. Some of these god names appeared in Kassite personal names and will be heard of later among the Battle-ax People who went to India. There is some indication that the Mitannians were not above a little missionary work, or at least not above applying a little diplomatic pressure in their gods' behalf. And so it was that Indo-European gods were honored, however briefly, however grudgingly, in several little cities of Syro-Palestine.

In 1460 B.C. or so, another Thutmose, the third of that name, went raging into Palestine on a punitive expedition. It was against "that contemptible enemy, Mitanni" that his wrath was primarily directed. The Hittites took the opportunity to attack Aleppo, a Syrian city loyal to Mitanni (they may have made common cause with Egypt). Thutmose III ravaged Mitanni lands though the two armies do not seem to have met. He then planted a triumphal stele on the east bank of the Euphrates and considered the Mitannian menace erased for good. For the next twenty-five years all the towns of Syro-Palestine were garrisoned with Egyptian troops. Only a few, usually, but so feared were they that there was not a sign of rebellion.

Mitanni was down but not out. She arose from this period of eclipse stronger than ever, took charge once again of her federated cities in northern Syria, and extended her influence southward. Next to Egypt she was the most powerful nation in the ancient world.

Pharaohs after Thutmose III felt secure in their dominions and sent fewer and fewer armies on parade through the vassal states. Eventually the fourth Thutmose entered into a treaty relationship with Mitanni, agreeing not to meddle with the states of northern Syria if Mitanni would stay out of southern Palestine. He also took to wife a Mitannian princess, who became mother to the next Pharaoh. This one, too, married a Mitannian princess, though not as chief wife of his heart. In the two royal families there was suddenly a good deal of shared affection as well as shared inheritance.

Not affection enough, however, to send Egypt to the rescue of Mitanni in her hour of need. In 1370 B.C., when the Hittites sacked Wassuggani, Egypt's current Pharaoh was otherwise occupied, and Mitanni became a vassal state to Hatti. Assyria then took her own independence.

By 1200 B.C. both Mitannians and Hurrians in Syro-Palestine had disappeared from political prominence—though Hurrians still in the hill land around Lake Van were later (around 900 B.C.) to build a kingdom for themselves, the Kingdom of Urartu. In the Jordanian hills sometime after 1200 B.C., Hebrews newly returned to their "promised land" after years of desert wandering prepared to battle for that land. Philistines were pushing inland from the sea. And along the coast, the merchant cities—and their Semitic merchant princes—continued business as usual. What of the old ways remained? Very little. Myths and stories which were popular among city folk of the coast sometimes show odd resemblances to the later tales from Greece. One recounts an event for all the world like the siege of Troy, a battle begun for love of a beautiful woman. Heroes of tales on both sides of the Mediterranean are alike in being musicians as well as soldiers. Is this simply an instance of ideas traveling from one storyteller to the next? Or has it something to do with the Maryannu and a dim and distant steppe homeland shared with the Mycenaean Greeks?

However faint their cultural contribution to the heritage of the

Middle East, in one way at least Mitanni affected the tides of history which washed the lands of those times. Scholars think it may have been in northern Mesopotamia or northern Syria that the light, spoke-wheeled chariot was invented. From somewhere in this area the Hyksos army, led by Maryannu, drove just such vehicles into helpless Egypt. Now the land in these parts is open and flat, nicely suited to chariot racing, which was a sport the Mitannian Maryannu adored. No one was better at it. No one bred better racing horses than the Mitannians. Everywhere, for every royal stable, they were in demand. It was a Mitannian with an Indo-European name (Kikuli—another version of the Luwian Kukun found on the Byblos obelisk) who wrote the only known treatise of that period on horse breeding, training, and racing, and charioteering in general though he wrote it in the Hurrian language, the numerals he used were the same as the Sanskrit numerals to be used later in India by the Battle-ax Aryans. Typically, the treatise was uncovered in Hatti, where Kikuli had no doubt been employed to train the Hittite chariotry.

Mitannian and Hyksos Maryannu fought in two-wheeled chariots, drawn by two horses, and carrying two men—one to drive and one to fight. So did the Egyptians, copying their conquerors. Hittite chariots, clumsy and heavy, carried three men. The strategy of chariot warfare was honed to a fine point everywhere. But by 1000 B.C. or so, chariots were out of style, relegated to taxi service, a means of transporting soldiers to the battlefield. Reliance was once again centered on the infantry. Men on horseback came into use as adjunct cavalry wings. Yet in 327 B.C. the Greek infantry of Alexander would face an Indian chariot charge. And three hundred years later the Romans in Britain would fight against an army of Celts driving wicker-basket chariots yoked to woolly little European ponies. So far an idea had traveled—and, on the fringes of events, so long did it live.

4. Hyksos

Freebooting in Egypt

Nothing ever seemed to change in Egypt. All the great themes and purposes of her existence were set in the first few centuries of nationhood. After that there were only small variations on a theme.

Unlike kaleidoscopic Mesopotamia, Egypt *could* stay the same, for she was protected on all sides—by deserts along the flanks, cataracts at one end, and sea at the other. And at the vital center was the Nile, whose ultimate gift Egypt was. A beneficent river was this gently flowing Nile. Nothing like the wild Euphrates or the even wilder Tigris. Every year, predictable as any clock, the river gradually swelled and rose in flood, watering the land and depositing the fertilizing silt. And it always happened exactly in the proper season, just before the winter's crops were due to be sown. Exactly right was the tilt of the land, so

that the water could drain off nicely, leaving no salty puddles behind. Exactly right was the cut of the banks for trapping the floodwaters in storage ponds. These irrigated the land in the dry season between floods and permitted the sowing of a second crop. Life may not have been easy in Egypt—not the way we think of ease—but it was by no means the grueling contest men fought in Mesopotamia. Unfailingly the sun god smiled. Unfailingly the river god made good his promise. Endless vistas, protective deserts, stretched out on either hand, and everything stayed exactly the same forever. At least until the Hyksos came.

In the beginning of its history, Egypt was divided into two lands: the northern delta, fruitful, advanced; the upriver south, strong, powerful. The king of the southern realm (Upper Egypt) with his assembled army defeated the Delta ruler, and henceforth the kings of Egypt wore the double crown, one white, one red, and were guided by the tutelary spirits of both lands. It is from this merging of the two lands that Egyptian history—both real and legendary—dates. The time: around 3100 B.C. Egypt's first picture writing commemorates that event.

It was not a collection of cities, this new, unified Egypt, but a string of towns and villages without the sense of civic identity which so marked Sumer. And, never having developed this political individuality, they were easily combined into one long ribbon nation whose people, like the people's gods, were one with the king as he was one with them. Perhaps it was the river, perhaps it was the king's ultimate divinity that bound the whole together and made it work. For between the king, the Pharaoh, as he was called, and the nation there was a mystic identity. The fertility of the land was in his care. His was the right to begin each year's sowing, each year's opening of the canals. His were the temples and the armies and all. In the king was centered the sacred *ma'at,* the harmony of land and realm and people. Since the king was divine, there was no need to make and publish laws, no need for councils or for public choice. The king saw all, knew all, and kept the good of all at heart.

It was in this period of mystic unity that the pyramids were built, those substantial mausoleums pointing heavenward wherein the kingly bodies rested—until grave robbers, whose love of gold outweighed their fear of punishment, disturbed them. These vast monuments were built by muscle power alone. There were no pulleys, no wheels, no draft animals, nothing to make the work easier for the armies of men called to labor for the Pharaoh. And they do not appear to have been slaves, whipped to their jobs. Quite willingly they devoted their efforts to the Pharaoh's tomb. For through that effort, through their closeness to the Pharaoh, perhaps they, too, would be granted the eternal life which was his alone to give.

It was, apparently, on these two rocks—the pyramids and the Pharaoh's monopoly regarding the afterlife—that the Old Kingdom came to an end. The economy sagged under the weight of the one, and men's resentment erupted because of the other. It is possible, too, that forays into Nubia had weakened the nation still further.

To the consternation of all, the mystic harmony departed the land. Nobody behaved as he should. The lower classes were brazen and insulting, the upper classes thievish and brutal. Worst of all, both king and kingship lost some of their ancient splendor. The high nobles ruled, each in his own domain. It was a time of chaos.

One writer of the era complained,

> The gentle man has perished
> But the violent man has access to everything!

When order was restored, things were much the same as ever they had been. No more pyramids were built, it is true, though cities of modest tombs mushroomed in the desert. For everyone and anyone now had a chance for life eternal if he could provide the proper embalming for his body and a final resting place, no matter how small. There was one other requirement. It was now necessary to have been good in life. After death, it was believed, Osiris, Lord of the Dead, would cause one's heart to be weighed against a feather. The heavy heart, the evil heart, would bring on one's bodily destruction. And the body's destruction brought obliteration to the soul. Never again to see the blessed sun, to sail on the Nile, to rejoice in the company of gods and men. Unthinkable! No wonder men began inscribing on their tomb walls such sentiments as these:

> There was no citizen's daughter whom I misused, there was no widow whom I afflicted, there was no peasant whom I evicted. . . . There was none wretched in my community, there was none hungry in my time. . . . I did not exalt the great man above the small man in anything that I gave.

This period of concern with goodness we know as Egypt's Middle Kingdom. It ended about 1800 B.C. and was followed soon after by the invasion from Palestine. It is true, of course, that certain internal, certain dynastic weaknesses gave the intruders their chance. But it is unlikely that even a strong Egypt, well armed and well led, could have resisted successfully. The intruders hurtled down upon the Egyptian troops in chariots drawn by fast horses. (Old-fashioned Egypt was not even using solid-wheeled carts.) They wielded strange and effective weapons—bronze battle-axes and composite bows—and they were protected with body armor. Their battle tactics were strange to the Egyptians. Worst of all, the fortresses they quickly built were impregnable. Pharaoh's armies quailed and fled south.

Hyksos—*hikau khasut*—the Egyptians called them, "rulers of foreign lands." And it seems certain that at the core of this much-mixed army led by Maryannu coalesced. To this were attracted all the dis-groups of them had been filtering into Syro-Palestine, establishing themselves, and consolidating their gains. Eventually a well-disciplined army led by Maryannu coalesced. To this were attracted all the dis-affected city folk of Syro-Palestine, the disinherited, the desert men hungry for spoil. Throughout the coastal corridor and into upper Mesopotamia the Maryannu built their great fortresses, some of them a thousand yards to a side. The walls of these fortresses were made of stone and pounded earth, their outer edges sloping down into wide moats. Whether this sort of sloping construction was intended as a defense against enemy chariots or against battering rams no one can say. Throughout Palestine the Maryannu made graves and left their dead behind, buried often with horses, chariots, jewelry, and battle-axes.

The humiliated Egyptians understandably thought of the invaders as despicable barbarians who demanded tribute while making a mockery of all things Egyptian. They could not even write about their subjugation until years after the dishonor had been erased. Then an Egyptian queen was to say:

> I have restored that which was ruined. I have raised up that which had formerly gone to pieces, since the Asiatics were in the midst of Avaris of the Delta, and vagabonds in their midst, overthrowing what had been made, for they ruled without Re. . . .

Impartial observers on the scene might not have found the Hyksos rulers quite so bad as all that. Trade did not cease with their coming. Temple worship was not disrupted. The Hyksos even chose Seth, one of the Egyptian gods, to represent them. True, he was something of a devil figure to the Egyptians, but since the gods were endowed with natures as changeable as those of human beings, the Hyksos must have

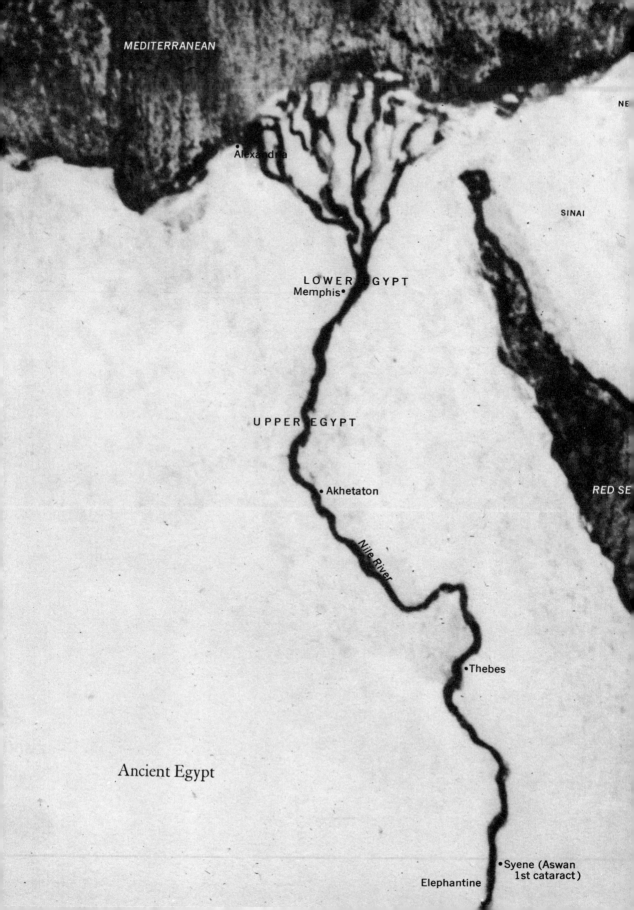

found something lovable about him. Scribal schools were continued as before, and some important scientific works were copied at Hyksos behest. The new rulers even permitted the old dynastic line to continue a shadow kingdom in the south. And some Egyptians, at least, were not averse to coexistence. As one group of courtiers told the shadow Pharaoh:

> ... we are at ease holding our [part of] Egypt. Elephantine is strong, and the midland is with us. ... Men till for us the finest of their land; our cattle are grazing in the Delta. Spelt is sent for our swine. Our cattle are not taken away, and there is no attack on [us]. ... He [the Hyksos king] holds the land of the Asiatics, we hold Egypt. But [whoever] comes to land and [attack us], we will oppose him.

But the shadow Pharaoh, the then Prince of Thebes, could not be content. The new rulers were imposing taxes *he* should impose. From their fortresses in the Delta they ruled an empire of which Egypt was only a part. Imagine! Great Egypt—a part! Throughout their empire the Hyksos were circulating scarabs, seal stamps of official business, marked with strange spiral symbols no self-respecting Egyptian would dream of using. Worse yet, a good many objects of Egyptian art were being appropriated by Palestinian soldiers on their way home.

The Prince of Thebes bided his time as any number of his predecessors had done (Hyksos rule lasted nearly two hundred years). He put up with the tribute. He even put up with insulting notes sent down from the Delta, such as the one in which a Hyksos Pharaoh complained that the bellowing of the Theban hippopotami disturbed his slumber. (Over five hundred river-miles lie between the Delta and Thebes!)

At last the Egyptian forces were ready, and the Prince of Thebes attacked. Bit by bit, mile by mile, the Hyksos tide was rolled back. The cause was not won without long effort. It took a year to reduce the

Delta fortresses and three years to conquer Sharuhen, the Hyksos center in the Negev. Palestinian allies of the Hyksos resisted as best they could, but the Egyptians had learned their bitter lessons well. By the mid-1400s B.C. not one of the hated Maryannu was left west of the Euphrates—at least, none with the least degree of importance. Eastward lay Mitanni.

Perhaps it is not too farfetched to think of Mitannian and Hyksos Maryannu as one and the same, with Mitanni simply marking the last of the Hyksos dominions in the Middle East. This would explain her continuing efforts to challenge Egypt and bring the little Palestinian states back into the fold.

Now at last things were different in Egypt—in outlook if in nothing else. Her people were turned to face the world beyond the Nile. They no longer felt safe, secure, protected, and they were never to feel so again, even with Palestine held as a buffer against the east. Nevertheless they had an empire to manage as best they could.

During this period—the time of the New Kingdom—these figures stand out: the Thutmoses I and III, conquering heroes who won and extended the empire; Hatshepsut, the queen who consolidated it; Akhnaton, the heretic who almost lost it all; and Rameses II, the wily braggart who put it back together again.

Hatshepsut had to struggle for her throne—to get it and to keep it. First of all, she was widely resented, for, although the royal line descended through the female (brothers married sisters in Egypt, largely to keep the throne in the family), a female Pharaoh was not exactly received with enthusiasm. Hatshepsut took care to dress as a king, to *be* a king, and most of her statues are equipped with the royal goatee. The few which portray her as a queen reveal a frail and girlish creature. No martinet, she. Yet, she did keep her nephew and coruler, the redoubtable Thutmose III, under virtual lock and key. And, since

she lived and reigned for some time, his impatience is understandable. When Thutmose did come into his own, he made sure to knock down or deface all the statues of Hatshepsut that could be found, and then set out to show the Palestinians who was boss.

Akhnaton, who followed Hatshepsut exactly a century later, in 1369 B.C., was not a well man. He suffered, it is believed, from epilepsy. And besides, he was something of a saint. Nevertheless, he did manage to marry the incomparable Nefertiti. Some say she was his sister, some, a Mitannian princess. In any case, though naturalism in art was the vogue in Akhnaton's time (he didn't mind having all his worst features accentuated!), nothing could alter Nefertiti's beauty, which survives for us to admire.

Akhnaton dedicated himself totally to religious reform. He ignored the army, resigned his title as commander-in-chief to a commoner general. He tried to obliterate all other gods but his own (Aton—the sun's disk) and impoverish their priesthoods into the bargain. He built a new capital city—Akhetaton, city of the horizon of Aton—in the ruins of which, thousands of years later, the diplomatic correspondence of the Middle East would be uncovered.

Distracted by all his new and absorbing interests, Akhnaton failed to mind the empire, and it slowly began to decay. Desert tribesmen harried the Palestinian kinglets tributary to Egypt. And they had not only the nomads to contend with, but their own rebellious subjects as well. Letter after letter they sent to Akhnaton, begging for help. No help was forthcoming. Neither was there help for Mitanni, which went down under the might of Hatti.

At last Akhnaton died (perhaps by poisoning), to be succeeded in turn by two boy kings and their wives, Akhnaton's eldest daughters. The last one, Tutankhamon, half-brother to the heretic, renounced Aton, died early, and is famous only because grave robbers overlooked his tomb, leaving us all his treasure intact. But he could hardly have had anything to do with *that*. His wife tried vainly to perpetuate the dynasty. She wrote to the powerful Hittite king (he who had trounced Mitanni), asking for one of his sons in marriage. For she would not, she said, marry one of her own subjects (or perhaps be forcibly married to someone she loathed). The Hittite king was amazed but duly sent a son to Egypt, where he was promptly killed. Savage reprisals were then taken on the Egyptian borders, but for what? The young man was lost, and so was the sad little queen. She was hurriedly married to an old but important priest and sent away somewhere to vanish from history.

Egyptian generals then took the throne, whether they had a right to it or no. They quelled the desert raiders and got the army back into shape. The son of one of them, Rameses II, had dreams of glory. He set out to conquer the Hittites and very nearly got himself beaten in the process. He was able to secure a sensible peace treaty (marrying a Hittite princess to seal the bargain, just as Thutmose IV had once done to seal a similar treaty with Mitanni). The agreement was reached only because both Assyria and the harrying Sea People were growing strong. But to read Rameses's account of the war, one would never know that. He was his own best press agent and built one whole temple just to boast about his "victory." Modern science has only recently managed to preserve this monument from the rising waters of the newly built Aswan Dam.

After Rameses II, Egypt began that long decline both of soul and of substance that was to last longer than most nations' entire histories.

The foreign invaders came in droves now. First Assyria, then Persia, then Alexander with his Greek armies. Last of all came Rome. With the death of its last ruler, the fabulous Cleopatra (who preferred snake bite to the humiliation of a Roman triumph), Egypt became just another imperial province, as she had once been under the Hyksos.

Beyond spurring the reach for empire, the Hyksos left little mark on Egypt. In the long run, Egypt herself has had less impact on the West than was once supposed. She was not, after all, the world's first literate civilization, and her contributions were more in the realm of elaboration and refinement than in outright invention.

The elegance, balance, and repose of Egyptian art were ultimately to shape the style of Greek art. Even today the figures in Egyptian paintings and the faces carved in stone speak to us over the millennia. There is about them still something fresh, something eternally modern, as though they might find themselves as much at home in this world as in their own.

Egypt's strongest influence on the character of the Western world came via religion. Actually, the Egyptian concept of the soul and of the afterlife found its way into the religious thinking of many ancient peoples. So did the Egyptian notion of the duality, yet essential oneness, of good and evil. Faithful Mother Isis, sorrowing for her slain lord, pinning her hopes on the son who would avenge him, was worshiped in many lands. Rome did her honor far into Christian times, and it is not inconceivable that some of her attributes were incorporated into the image of the Blessed Mother Mary.

But it was on the Hebrews that Egyptian religion had its greatest effect. Some had apparently come into Egypt with the Hyksos. Once there, they warmed to Egyptian wisdom and Egyptian moral precepts. Some are carried over directly into the Book of Proverbs. Compare, for example, these few fragments:

The Teaching of Amen-em-ope	*Proverbs*
Beware of robbing the poor, And of oppressing the afflicted.	Rob not the poor, for he is poor, Neither oppress the lowly in the gate
A scribe who is skillful in his business Findeth himself worthy to be a courtier.	A man who is skillful in his business Shall stand before kings.
Toil not after riches; If stolen goods are brought to thee They remain not over the night with thee; They have made for themselves wings like geese And have flown into the heavens.	Toil not to become rich And cease from thy dishonest gain; For wealth maketh to itself wings Like an eagle that flieth heavenward.
Give thine ears, hear the words that are said, Give thine heart to interpret them.	Apply thine heart unto instruction And thine ears to the words of knowledge.

It was the Egyptian genius to perceive the many in the one, and the one in the many—one First Principle expressed in countless forms. Eventually this principle came to be embodied in the sun itself, and eventually there came Akhnaton, who worshiped *only* the One, the sun's disk, Aton, excluding the many who had formerly shared in his glory. He was proclaimed, this Aton, to be not simply a local god, and not even an Egyptian god, but the god of all mankind. The Hebrews were profoundly affected by this teaching. In the beauty of their Psalms can be heard many an echo of Egyptian hymns to the sun.

The Aton Hymn	*Psalm 104*
When thou settest in the western horizon,	Thou makest darkness and it is night,
The land is in darkness like death	
. . .	
Every lion comes forth from his den;	Wherein all the beasts of the forest creep forth.
All creeping things, they sting.	The young lions roar after their prey.
At daybreak, when thou arisest in the horizon . . .	The sun ariseth, they get them away . . .
Thou drivest away the darkness . . .	
Men awake and stand upon their feet . . .	Man goeth forth unto his work,
All the world, they do their labor.	And to his labor until the evening.
How manifold are thy works!	O Jahweh, how manifold are thy works!
They are hidden from man's sight.	
O sole god, like whom there is no other,	
Thou hast made the earth according to thy desire.	In wisdom hast thou made them all; The earth is full of thy riches.

The second tide of Egyptian religious influences came later and flowed directly into the main stream of Christianity. They came by way of Egyptian Alexandria, where Greek and Egyptian and Hebrew and Roman ideas met and were mingled. Alexandria became in time the seat of learning for the Byzantine world—the nursery of Christian doctrine and the center of Christian heresy. It was here, and in the deserts beyond, that the Egyptian obsession with piety and with preparation for the hereafter—so characteristic of its helpless, hopeless later years—found expression through Christian ascetics, hermits who devoted their lives to solitude and self-punishment. The monastic life, with all the profusion of priories, abbeys, and convents which later sprang up all over medieval Europe, had its beginning, too, in Egypt.

In time the Arabs came with yet another religion, and the Egyptians changed once again. Egypt gave a dynasty to the Moslem world, and she continued to bear the great old name, but the glory had flown. Gone was her language, gone her Pharaohs, "kings of the great house," gone her ancient mystery, her magic strangeness. Remaining only was the awe of age, great age that stretches the still-living present back into the mists of time.

5. Aryans

Swallowed Up in India

Of all the Battle-ax People who invaded sown lands and encountered city folk, none tried harder than the Aryans to hang on to old ways of life. What they found in India they thought to change to suit themselves. What they found changed them instead. For India with its heat, its old civilization, its timeless, languid dreaming proved to be a kind of flypaper which in the end swallowed the Aryan fly.

Arya simply means "freeborn." Kings of the Medes and Persians, as well as the Battle-ax charioteers who went to India, were proud to call themselves Aryan. Much of the Iranian Plateau, including the modern country of Afghanistan, has been called Aryana. And "Iran" itself is just another spelling of the name for the Aryan home. And yet resemblances between the languages once spoken on the plateau,

what is known of Hittite, and the names and numerals from Kassite and Mitannian sources tell us plainly of a still more ancient common home on the far side of the Caucasus.

It must have been sometime around 1500 B.C. that the Aryans moved down from the plateau and into India, leaving their Aryan cousins, the Medes and Persians, behind in the hinterland. They were closely related, these cousins. The traditions of all three reveal a common preoccupation with cattle. Cattle were food and wealth, honor and religious sacrifice. The very word for war in Sanskrit, the language of the Aryans, means "desire for cows." Medes, Persians, and Aryans were charioteers, lovers of fast horses—those royal animals which could be sacrificed only at the installation of great chieftains. The most important social unit for both people was the clan (in Persian, *zantu;* in Sanskrit, *janas*), and this must have been true for most Battle-ax folk (in Latin, for instance, we find *genus,* in Greek, *genos,* though we get the English *clan* from yet another root, from a word which means "to plant").

The Aryans loved to sing and dance and fight and brag, preferably in epic verse. When they stopped to build, one hut was always a club for men only, a place where warriors forgathered to gamble and drink.

The very model of the model Aryan gentleman was Indra, the god of war, but also (perhaps appropriating the old sky father's attributes) the god of the rain and the heavens. One of the ancient Aryan hymns addresses him thus:

> Thou, Indra, art born from power, strength, and vitality.
> Thou, Bull, art really a bull.
> Thou, Indra, carriest in thine arms thy glorious shining weapon
> Sharpening it with thy strength.

Indra's weapon was a thunderbolt. He was known and admired among all the chariot invaders along the Zagros range—Mitannians, Kassites,

Persians, Aryans. (Not the Hittites, to be sure, who had converted to the religious forms of their new homeland.) Also known to Mitannians, Persians, and Aryans were the twin Nasatyas, the healer or physician gods; Mitra, god of the sacred contract; and Varuna, god of divine order, Mitra's second self. Only to Varuna, of all the Indo-Aryan gods, were petitions for forgiveness addressed:

> Our fathers' sins loose from us, loose those which we have committed of ourselves.

> What sin we have ever committed against an intimate, O Varuna, against a friend or companion at any time, a brother, a neighbor, or a stranger, that, O Varuna, loose from us.

If Indra personified the worst in Indo-Aryan nature, surely Varuna symbolized the best. No rock or tree or temple confined him or Mitra (or any of the Aryan gods, for that matter). Like the gods of desert Semites, they were nongeographical, and their home was boundless as the sky.

> The two sovereigns . . . Mitra and Varuna, are the swift lords of heaven and earth. In shining clouds ye come to the sound of our praise. . . . Duly ye rule over the whole world.

Kassite names do not perpetuate these gods, but a certain Luristanian plaque, attributed to Kassite influence, seems to honor their likenesses. Important to the Kassites were the Maruts (war gods—*maryas,* young charioteers—led by Indra), Suryas (the sun's self), and Burias (the wind)—all of them additional divinities of the Aryan pantheon. In Aryan India and also in Persia the fire god was Agni (he lives still in our word *ignite*). Sacred, too, was the liquor that made men drunk with the lust for battle or the exaltation of the gods—*haoma* to the Persians, *soma* to the Aryans.

How did they come into India—these soma-swilling, battle-happy charioteers? Their route is not clearly marked by archaeological remains, though there are a few signposts here and there. In the hills of southern Pakistan there have been unearthed old villages destroyed and then reoccupied by people who had horses (previously unknown in the area), people who made great circles of stone bisected by avenues pointing east and west. Were these people worshipers of the round sun in its rising and setting? Some specialists have thought so. Further on, in other village remains, have been found horse bells, stone-mounded graves, and shaft-hole battle-axes. And there are evidences of destruction by fire all along a trail leading ever southward until one comes to a drop into a wide plain and the great river which has cut it from the plateau. We call this river the Indus, a name given it by Aryan wanderers who (as E. D. Phillips suggests) must have held dear the memory of another river on the far side of the Caucasus—a river draining into the Black Sea and called Sindhu.

The footloose Aryans left few traces of their journey, but the people they encountered in the plain have provided an archaeological treasure-trove. For they were builders, sophisticated urban folk, and the cities they made were like no other cities of their time or any time thereafter right up to the present. No helter-skelter jumble of buildings were here, no maze of crooked lanes. These cities were planned. Some ancient urban engineer laid them out on a grid pattern of broad straight avenues, narrow straight streets, and alleys also straight or sometimes deliberately jogged to break the wind whistling through. Fired brick was used everywhere, and everywhere by master masons. Houses were spacious, built around courtyards, and equipped with bathrooms. These connected to a truly elaborate sewerage system punctuated here and there by neat inspection holes.

One finds no palaces in these cities and no temples either. Each city was, instead, dominated by a high-walled mound on which were built a granary, a pool, brick-lined and coated with pitch to make it waterproof, and buildings with cubicle-like rooms and baths. Was this place meant to be a citadel? A warehouse-reservoir? A government house? A public bath? Taking into account the sort of ritual bathing common in later Indian days, one would be more inclined to give the pool religious rather than utilitarian significance. Was the mound structure a temple then? Perhaps. We do not know.

Because the cities of the Indus (now part of modern Pakistan) were so well planned and, seemingly, built from scratch, with no long period of development in evidence, some archaeologists have thought them to be offshoots of Sumer. Seal stones from the Indus, dated to 2300 B.C., have been found in Sumerian cities. Clearly the two civilizations were in communication; possibly they were trading partners.

Certainly the initial farming impetus—the knowledge of wheat, barley, and domesticated animals—came from Neolithic centers north and west of the Indus and traveled down through the fertile, hidden valleys of Afghanistan. Other ideas came, too: that of pottery and its decoration, of the fired brick, and of the inevitable mother goddess, lovingly made of clay. Down toward India, however, something new apparently happened to the goddess and to ideas about her. She lost much of her old Anatolian fat and with it a great deal of her good nature. Goddess figures of the villages above the Indus plain have frightening beaked faces, death heads really. They are often coated with a red-lead coloring that in later Indian days would always signify blood. And they are to be found set atop ceremonial platforms at the mouths of brick-lined drains leading nowhere in particular. In later times, says Professor Joseph Campbell, such drains bore the blood of human sacrifice to the mother goddess, in no day or way given greater honor than in India. These same figures and these same sorts of drains are to be found in the two great Indus cities. To be sure, other religious figures were made there, figures neither so frightening nor so crude. Some were made just for fun and bear no religious connotations. Not a great many of either sort, however, for metals and stones had to be imported into the alluvial Indus plain.

The Indus civilization was advanced and widespread. Its influence covered an enormous triangular section of the subcontinent, a thousand miles to a side. It had two proud capitals, Harappa, upstream on the tributary Ravi, and Mohenjo-Daro, downstream on the Indus. Almost as old as Sumer and Egypt, the Indus civilization dates back at least to 2600 B.C. It also had writing. Examples of the strange Indus script are to be found primarily on seal stones adorned with beautiful animal figures. Some four hundred symbols—probably idea signs—have been isolated in all. What they meant we do not know. And so we cannot

Aryan Invasions of India

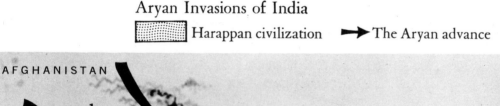

Harappan civilization ➤ The Aryan advance

interpret with conviction the goddesses, buildings, or art forms. We can only guess.

We are not even sure how the great civilization met its end. The Aryans have long been held responsible. Now it seems that the real villain of the piece (for Mohenjo-Daro, if not Harappa) was mud and marsh water which slowly rose when an earth upheaval dammed the Indus. The citizens tried valiantly to rise above it—literally. Brick by brick they lifted the city on parapets and platforms. But the standard of living sank yearly until mere hovels were being built atop the accumulated ruins of beautiful old houses. Finally the city was deserted altogether, and the fall of the capital apparently precipitated the decay of the whole civilization.

And yet the incoming Aryans cannot be let off scot-free. Battle-axes and pins very like those made over the Caucasus have been found in the city ruins. Found, too, have been the skeletons of massacred families left to lie where they had fallen. Aryan tradition exults in the toppling of walled cities and the killing of Dasyus, their dark-skinned inhabitants. Indra himself is called "fort destroying." He may have been a dam-destroyer as well. "Indra . . . let loose to flow the seven rivers," sing the hymns. *Some* of the Indus cities between 1500 and 1200 B.C. must have suffered attack as well as natural catastrophe. The name of one such preserved in Sanskrit tradition is Hari-Yupuya. Harappa, perhaps? There is no way of knowing for sure. The Indus civilization gives us plenty of bricks and no words at all, at least none that we can read and understand. The Aryans, on the other hand, give us words and little else. And from neither can exact history be drawn.

The Aryan words, along with the old traditions they preserve, live in four collections of hymns called Vedas, a name which comes from a root that means "to see" (*video*—the word for what we see on our TV screens—is a sprig from the same root). In the hymns the various gods are praised, adored, thanked for destroying property and driving out the native population, always spoken of in the most derogatory terms. Dasyus, they are called, black (*krishna*), noseless (*anasas*), and cowardly, worshiping "dog-faced" goddesses in rites which the charioteers found repulsive in the extreme. All the local deities were immediately dismissed as demons to be feared and opposed. To make the distinction complete between the two peoples and their gods, the Aryans drew a color line called *varna*.

There can be little doubt that the Aryans did indeed dispossess the folk in residence along the Indus as their traditions insist. Indo-European languages are today spoken largely in the northern parts of India, while in the south one hears non-Indo-European speech. It seems probable also that the people native to India were indeed darker than the invaders. It is thought that some natives belonged to the same race as that of the invaders, though looking rather more Greek or Italian than Slavic or Swiss. Others were possibly members of a mixed racial group rather like that to which the natives of Australia belong. One thing is clear. The aboriginal Indians cannot have been as repulsive as the Vedic hymns claim. Neither can varna have been very effective in keeping the groups apart, because the population of India today is a kaleidoscope of color in all classes, high and low. And the mixing began soon after the invasion.

Preservation of the soma-bibbing, hard-fighting, snobbish character that was the Aryan knight is entirely due to people who in the beginning probably were not Aryan at all. The charioteers had of old been without special priests or temples or any sort of ritual apparatus. Family fathers, clan fathers had officiated at the fire sacrifices, and no doubt many of the Vedic hymns were songs made on the spot by warriors drunk with soma or battle. And then somehow, from somewhere, came priests, called Brahmans ("those who pray"), who committed the songs to memory, froze them in their original spoken form, and passed them down from Brahman to Brahman, unchanged and unchanging in word and tone from that day to this. Even when alphabetic writing came to India in about 700 B.C., the hymns were not committed to paper; they were considered far too sacred for that. (Not until a few hundred years ago were the Vedas in their ancient Sanskrit form published at last.) Brahmans began to act as well as memorize, officiating at all ceremony of whatever sort. They were everywhere.

Where had they come from, these Brahmans? Of the founders of the major priestly clans mentioned in the Vedas, only one is Aryan by name. Most Brahman clan fathers claimed to be descended from a god, to have been found in lightning bolts or born of jars in which Mitra and Varuna had deposited life. Pretty tales, says historian D. D. Kosambi, to disguise the simple fact of intermarriage between Aryan and Dasyu. Or were these jar-born Brahmans perhaps scions of the pre-Aryan Indus priesthood, proud but canny intellectuals of the old order making their peace with the new?

Whoever they were, they began to take hold. Soon they were not only preserving tradition, they were making it. Always the sacred words were slanted to put the Brahmans in the best possible light. Varna was no longer a color bar but a convenient way of keeping the Aryan warrior, Aryan farmer-tradesman, and the Dasyu laborer each in his own place, practicing his own skill, confined to his proper sphere of knowledge, marrying only his own kind. (A very late Vedic hymn sanctifies the arrangement.) And all the while the Brahmans (now considered more Aryan than the original invaders) exalted their rank and collected their perquisites. These were considerable. The Brahman was free from taxation or molestation of any sort and loaded with gifts, fees, lands, and honors. ("Him, I hold, is a king of men who first introduced the fee," sings a Vedic priest.)

The Brahman was expected, however, to spend twelve years of his life at the feet of a teacher, from whom he learned all the sacred texts, committing them to memory. In these Brahmanical "schools" commentaries on the Vedas began to appear and, with them, subtle changes in the old tradition. The gods were slowly merged, their characters and attributes shifted about, until at last they were no longer all-powerful but were superseded by the Brahmans themselves, who were greater than gods. In one story (repeated faithfully along with all the rest) great Indra is nearly devoured by a monster, creature of a mighty Brahman. He is rescued only just in the nick of time and survives to take revenge. Alas, there is no sweetness in the triumph, for Indra has sinned. He has destroyed a Brahman.

Already the flypaper was winning.

Aryans who had settled along the Indus kept to their old herding ways and their old beliefs, breaking into small chiefdoms and fighting one another. A Chinese traveler in the seventh century B.C. was shocked at their barbarous habits and put his comments into writing. Some of these northwestern Aryans, however, had rather early begun to move from the Indus River system to the wetter, more jungly Ganges system. It may have been in pursuit of metals or adventure. Whatever their reasons, the result was a new world. Rice, a gift from Southeast Asia, was grown in the Ganges basin instead of wheat, and the old herding way took a back seat to agriculture. Trading brought wealth in something other than cattle. Not only copper but iron was found in the new environment—iron for cutting down the trees and putting cities in their stead. Again—cities. Delhi—Benares—Kosambi—and many others.

With the building of these cities, ideas changed. The old tribal lines, the old caste lines were not so rigidly drawn. Aryans willingly married the native folk of the forest (called Nagas because they identified with Naga, the cobra god). The new cities and their folk eventually consolidated into kingdoms, bigger, more complex, more various than the clans and tribal units of the Indus Aryans. The traditional warrior with sword for hire was needed a good deal less than the humble foot soldier or the bureaucrat toiling in the network of government. And it was not Vedic hymns but the formulae of statecraft that were needed to make things work. Eventually such formulae were compiled and put into writing—as cold-blooded a list of ways to train, curb, and kill a prince, of ways to subvert a rival kingdom, and of ways to enrich one's own state as have ever been devised anywhere.

If traditional rule came into question, so did traditional religion. Dissident, rebellious thinkers retired to the forest, there to meditate on the meaning of life. Neither old gods nor Brahmans, they began to feel, had the power to deepen that meaning. At the heart of meaning was the creative One, Brahma (a name which seems to derive from *Brahmanaspati*—"Lord of Prayer"—surely a personification ultimately of priestly invention). And all that mattered was Brahma, the individual human soul, and the longing life after life after life for an eventual union of soul with the One. In order to realize the One, some thinkers punished their bodies, did without food or sleep, thinking thus to free spirit from the bonds of flesh.

One man preached the middle way. Buddha was an Aryan son of the warrior caste who renounced both pleasure and punishment of the body. Real peace, he said, was to be gained only through detachment from emotion, and detachment was to be gained simply through right thinking, right behavior, right choices. The rules could work for everyone, warriors and wealthy men, laborers and kings. The correct performance of ritual and rigorous strict obedience to the strictures of caste could not of themselves produce right behavior. Better for

every man to have enough to eat and enough worthwhile work to occupy him than to worry about his religious duties, which were, in any case, an illusion. Making sure that people had food and work in plenty was the king's responsibility, he said.

Buddha's teachings were simple, direct, addressed not to the favored few but to everyone. They were teachings for the world, and as such they spread rapidly and took hold. Not, however, in the palaces of kings. It was not that kings did not listen to Buddha and offer patronage. It was just that religion and statecraft were considered worlds apart (in most modern states they still are).

Certainly centuries were to pass before religion and politics moved closer together in India. During those centuries the Ganges kingdoms were consolidated into the Mauryan Empire. Then, in 327 B.C., Alexander the Great raided the Indus region, weakening the tribal

Aryans, leaving them open to attack by Mauryan soldiers. Soon they, too, were added to the Mauryan state, which covered the northern third of the Indian subcontinent.

Around 270 B.C. the Mauryans produced a true philosopher-king. This was the great Ashoka. Though a Buddhist, he revered and supported all religious orders, protected the rights of all peoples and tribes, from the simplest food-gathering folk to the rich merchants of the towns. Each group had its advocate in court.

This golden age was not to last. Slowly, under Ashoka's descendants, the empire fragmented once more into smaller kingdoms. Notions of rule were keyed less to social need than to the myriad religious notions tenaciously held by myriads of villagers and starving poor in the cities. Slowly the will to move and change, the energy for military conquest and moral innovation dimmed and were lost in the dreaming forest world which had given them birth.

Influences flowing from India to the West have borne the stamp of that forest world, of solitary forest sages who thought deeply about the meaning of life. By many a roundabout route their ideas found their way into Greek philosophy. Indians were never much interested in history or logic, and they were able to accept with equal respect all myths, all cosmologies, all religious ideas, however contradictory. Abstraction in any form was the Indian long suit, so it comes as no surprise to learn that algebra and the notion of zero—perfect nothingness—were invented by Indians and came west by way of Arabia. For the most part, however, Indian theology and Indian codes have had their greatest impact in the East—specifically in Southeast Asia and Tibet—where they met and were challenged by culture patterns coming from China. It was here that Buddha's teachings took firmest root, here that they were to be preserved long after Buddhism in India had quite died away.

For die it did. There, Buddha, who had staunchly resisted all discussions about the gods, was himself made first a god, then a succession of godlets, then an incarnation of another deity. The inventive
Brahmans were never at a loss for incarnations.

It was by way of incarnations that the old pre-Aryan gods finally
thrust the Vedic deities out of first place altogether. Long before, in
the early commentaries on the Vedas, the Brahmans had experimented
with creator gods under different names. The forest sages had given
enduring meaning to abstract Brahma, the One, so as personified Brahmā
he was given pride of place in the evolving Brahman pantheon. Co-
regnant with him was Vishnu, the Preserver. Once an obscure, all-
purpose divinity in the Vedas, Vishnu came in time to occupy front
rank, still wearing his many faces. It was as an incarnation of Vishnu
that Buddha was drawn into the new fold, into Hinduism, as this
later religion of India was called. Another Vishnu incarnation accomplished the final triumph of the dispossessed Dasyus. His very
name proclaims the new order, for he was called Krishna, the Black
One, irresistibly beautiful to all females, of delightful temper and mood,
best loved of all the gods of India. He was, moreover, a charioteer, and
his weapon was the wheel-shaped discus, as shining and mighty as
Indra's lightning bolt. He was seen protecting the Nagas of the forest.
He also protected cattle from the depredations of Indra (now a figure
of villainy), protected them so thoroughly that cattle would never
again be killed in India and their flesh (once the delight of hungry
warriors) would become forbidden food.

The third member of the new Hindu trinity was Shiva, the De-
stroyer. Shiva was neither invented nor rearranged. Vedic now in name,
he was not Vedic in being, for he had been in India all along. He
was there when the Aryans came to the Indus, there on seal stones,
identifiable in pose and posture and costume, the same Shiva that men

would worship in later times. Shiva—Lord of the Beasts, Prince of Yogis, Lord of Benares (the Gangetic city where presumably his worship had been reintroduced). Shiva, whose wife was the terrible earth mother, lady of death who delighted in the blood of human sacrifice. Dancing Shiva, whose beautiful stone torso was found in Mohenjo-Daro, as graceful as his images today. Three-headed Shiva, who saw, who destroyed, and in destroying, created anew. Slowly, slowly, the added commentaries, preserved along with the old traditions, tell the tale.

The old Vedic gods are seen visiting Shiva on his mountain, dancing for him, amusing him, begging boons. Defiant Indra asks to be made as mighty a warrior as Shiva. Shiva agrees, but then repents of his gift and creates a monster which drives all the old gods from heaven and nearly conquers Vishnu. Only when they all approach Shiva humbly, begging for help, does he relent and destroy his creature with a disk so burning-bright that the gods are blinded and even Brahmā's beard is singed.

The Aryan warrior and his gods had come to India and there had been transformed into something other than what they were. The hero with his ax, symbol of the terrible, the fleeting but irresistible *now,* had been absorbed into the timeless forest world which endures and dreams, seeing individuals as passing shadows and one truth of as little value as another.

Indra, as Sir Mortimer Wheeler puts it, won the battle; Shiva won the war.

6. Persians

A Meeting of Minds

The years from 600 to 500 B.C. were fateful ones for religion in many places. This was the time of the great Buddha in India, of Confucius in China, of the beginnings of Greek philosophy, and in Persia, of Zoroaster. It was a time of questioning old gods and old ways and fashioning new ones.

The old gods in Persia we know largely by way of what Zoroaster had to say about them, and what he had to say was not at all flattering. By and large the roster of divinities was much the same as in Vedic India. In India, however, the invaders had been able to draw an ours-theirs, an Aryan-Dasyu, distinction in everything, certainly in terms of gods: ours—good, theirs—bad; ours—celestial, theirs—demons.

Among the Persians and their cousins the Medes, this kind of division was not possible. The Iranian homeland—before the descent into Mesopotamia's orbit, before the contacts with the big, bad city world—was Iranian through and through. From the Zagros Mountains north past the Caspian and on into the steppes beyond, everyone was much the same. Horse people, cattle people, mostly, with a few farmers settling in. They had the same language, same way of life. There were no ins, no outs.

Zoroaster made his own distinctions. There were things about the old ways that offended him deeply. He hated the ritual haoma (soma) drinking and the blood sacrifices of cattle. He hated the old gods, particularly Indra—that old reprobate, so embarrassingly, so barbarously human. In Zoroaster's books, Indra was demoted from godship and made to take his place among the demons. The frozen ritual into which Iranian religion had settled bothered Zoroaster, too. He objected to its monopoly by the Magi, a clan of hereditary priests who were running things to suit themselves as thoroughly as were the Brahmans in India.

He gathered his courage and preached reform. God is not fallible, petty, human, said Zoroaster. He is all goodness, all truth, all light. And He is not many but One. To symbolize this ultimate One Zoroaster merged the purest and most abstract, perhaps ultimately the most sacred of the Indo-Aryan pantheon, the joined gods whose eye (says the earliest Veda) was the shining sun: Agni, god of fire; Mithra (Vedic Mitra), god of the contract; and above all, Varuna, god of cosmic order. None of the old names was used, of course, or scarcely ever mentioned in other connections. All the old gods had been called *daevas* or perhaps *ahuras*—"our lords"—(*asuras* in Sanskrit), and so Zoroaster's divine merger became Ahuramazda, the Wise Lord, Lord of Truth and Light. Lord, too, of Good and Evil, spirits which Zoroaster described as having the power of choice, the power of will. "Evil Spirit," he said, "is wicked because he chooses to be so. Therefore must he be opposed by Good Spirit and by all men who follow truth and light." Those who followed Good Spirit, of course, followed the good religion, which we know as Mazdaism.

Zoroaster had little influence among his own small tribal group. ("A prophet is not without honor, save in his own country, and in his own house," as St. Matthew observed.) He was in fact actively disliked, especially among the local Magi, and was forced to flee to far-off Chorasmia (a steppe land near Bactria), where he found a more sympathetic chieftain who enjoyed listening while he preached.

The Persians (or Pars) were at this time mostly settled at the southern edge of the Iranian Plateau where it fronts what is now the Persian Gulf. They were fragmented—in the old steppe fashion— into many clans and tribal groups, sometimes friendly, sometimes hostile. About the biggest thing they had in common was a hatred of the Medes, in whose company they had originally crossed the Caucasus, probably sometime before 1000 B.C. The Medes, along with remnants of other Battle-ax groups, had been persuaded by the wily Babylonians to help shake loose the Assyrian hold on Mesopotamia and the Zagros region. The Babylonians had long despised the up-starts of the Tigris with their ruthless armies, their cruelties, and their annoying dreams of empire but had never been strong enough to do much about it. The Medes were better than their word. First they shook off Assyria and sent her Scythian allies galloping back over the Caucasus to the plains beyond. Then they utterly destroyed Assyria and reoccupied what had been Assyrian lands. In 612 B.C. they shared world power with decaying Egypt and Babylonia. But not for long.

Sometime around 580 B.C. an important marriage took place. Asty-ages, King of the Medes, gave his daughter's hand in marriage to an obscure prince of the Persian chiefly clan, the Achaemenid clan. It seems that Astyages, a cruel and superstitious man, had had dreams about this daughter (so the story goes), dreams in which her son-to-be became ruler of the East. Better, thought Astyages, to send her off to the Persians, who certainly posed no threat to Median rule. A grandson was duly born, and still Astyages was troubled by dreams. He tried to have the boy killed, but somehow young Cyrus escaped to make his grandfather's dreams come true. Partly through alliance with Babylonia, partly through appeals to avarice and appeals to pride, he managed to unite all the Persian tribes and led them to victory against the Medes. This was in 550 B.C.; more was yet to come. To Anatolia, to Babylonia, westward toward Egypt, and eastward to the gates of India Cyrus advanced. Within eleven years after his first gamble he had put together the largest empire in the world, and he had done so as much by decent and honorable treatment of his own and of conquered people as by superior battle tactics.

Whether or not Cyrus was a follower of Zoroaster, whether the new dispensation was yet (as it would later become) the official religion of the Achaemenid clan, we do not know. We do know that Cyrus worshiped Ahuramazda and was a very good man. It seems likely, too, that it was by way of Cyrus and his army that some rather new ideas came into the Hebrew religion and, through it, to the West.

The Jews had suffered mightily at the hands of Assyria and Babylonia. Many had been carried off captive into Mesopotamia, where they stayed until Cyrus arrived as conqueror and allowed them—even helped them—to go home again. It was at about this time or a little later that the Jews began to think and write about something new to them: a life after death of bliss or of pain according to one's deeds on earth and the judgment of the Most High. In times past not much thought had been devoted to the afterlife. It had been pictured as a

Persian Empire about 500 B.C.

dim, shadowy place—much like the early Greek Tartarus—to which all would go, whether good or bad in life. Real life, continuing life, was to be sought in the family, the People, the faith. Now ever since Zoroaster, Persians had believed in a judgment and an afterlife. This was not to be an infinite continuation of the everyday, nor was punishment simply extinction of the personality as in the old Egyptian conception. No. For the virtuous, bliss was to be found in a high place where ascending rings of glory brought the soul ever closer to union with the Lord of Light and his Bounteous Immortals. Even more vividly described was the House of the Lie, a place of fiery torment presided over by Evil Spirit, who tempted men to damnation. Eventually there was to be a final judgment and a general reuniting of bodies and souls. All these ideas made their way through Judaism and into Christianity as Heaven, Hell, the Angels, Satan, and the Last Judgment.

It was not only the Jews whom Cyrus honored and assisted. He was tolerant of all people (even Astyages) and of all religions everywhere. He claimed to want to restore captured gods and "make them happy." Certainly no conqueror was more tactful. In Babylon, for example, he was careful to call himself the King of Babylon, favored son of Marduk. Persia was mentioned only later in the string of titles, as a sort of afterthought.

Already by Cyrus's time, Mazdaism was not quite the religion as preached originally by Zoroaster. No sooner had he died than the old gods came trooping back into the Persian pantheon. Mithra began to pre-empt his old coequal role, and others were added as the need arose. And need there was. Ordinary folk had trouble comprehending Zoroaster's somewhat abstract theology and clung to the old ways. Fifty years after Cyrus's time, Herodotus (the Greek father of history) wrote an account of Persia and Persian religion without so much as a mention of Zoroaster. For Persian gods he listed Greek equivalents, with the exception of Mithra (whom he thought a female deity).

> . . . the Persians . . . do not think it lawful to make images, neither do they build altars or temples, charging them with folly who do such things. This, I suppose, is because they never regarded the gods as being of a nature like man's, as the Greeks do. . . . They call the whole circle of the sky by the name of Zeus. They sacrifice also to the sun, the moon, earth, fire, water, and the winds. These are their original gods . . .

During Cyrus's time and just after, a good deal of mixing went on. After all, Persia was now called upon to manage great numbers of unruly people, all speaking and writing and believing differently. They had to be consolidated into one going governmental concern.

In terms of political expertise, the Persians were little more advanced than the nomadic, tribal Scythians of the trans-Caucasan plains. It was necessary to borrow ideas, to pick up city ways fast. Said Herodotus: "No nation has ever been more ready than the Persians to admit foreign customs." They were not like the Egyptians, for instance, who, he said, "shrink from adopting the ways of the Greeks, and indeed, those of any other people whatsoever."

Cyrus never had time to do much personal borrowing. Most of his life was spent on horseback and in the field. He lost his life trying forcibly to incorporate some of the steppe nomads into the new empire. In later times Persians called him Father of His People. Cambyses, his son and successor, became The Master, so cruel and dominating was he. But Darius, who came next and who got the throne by guile, was called The Shopkeeper, because he knew the worth of everything and took care to get it for himself.

It was Darius who thoroughly organized the empire along Assyrian lines instead of trying personally to be all things to all people. The empire was divided into provinces (satrapies). These were ruled by members of the Persian nobility, most of whom felt strongly about their trusts. Darius saw that good roads were built, and he maintained an absolutely dependable system of communication (in Herodotus's description it sounds rather like the American Pony Express). The bulk of Mesopotamian court records and laws were codified and a regular judiciary set up. The laws were harsh, but they were fairly administered. (Whatever their faults, Persian kings demanded that judges be incorruptible.) Nothing, it seems, was so dreaded among Persians as being in debt or telling a lie. A gentleman's education (Herodotus tells us) consisted of instruction in three things and three things only: riding a horse, shooting a bow, and telling the truth. Surely this passion for truth was due to Persian religious tenets.

Persian art absorbed themes and techniques from every source. Darius lists in an inscription all the foreign artisans who worked on his palace at Persepolis. Even the image of Ahuramazda, which appeared in bas reliefs to hover over his head and over the heads of all Persian kings thereafter, looked much like Assur, patron god of the chief Assyrian city. The winged sun in which Ahuramazda stood was older still, having been used by Hittite and Mitannian kings to indicate the favor of the gods. With all its borrowing, however, the look of Persian art and architecture is unmistakably fresh and new, owing as much to the animal art of the steppes and of Luristan as to the city art of the river plain.

However discriminating the Achaemenid taste in art, however fine their religious ideals, they were fast becoming despots, Oriental style. Revenge for offending royalty was taken obliquely. Children were killed to punish their parents. Mothers were tortured to punish erring daughters. When Darius put down a revolt in Babylon, there was none of Cyrus's kindness shown to the inhabitants. Leading citizens were impaled and wealth was confiscated on a wholesale basis. Darius's son, Xerxes, who refused to make concessions to foreign sensibilities, did not even scruple to melt down the gigantic gold statue of Babylon's holy Marduk. Councils of nobles were called only to voice approval of a ruler's whim, and men disagreed at their peril. Even Ahuramazda was used to give the ruler extra importance, to add to his stature. Wrote Darius:

> The Great God is Ahuramazda who has created this earth, who has created yonder sky, who has created mankind, who has created welfare for man, who has made Darius king, the one king of many, one lord of many.

It would be only a short step to divinity, or something right next door.

In the matter of marriage, Persian kings did not stint themselves. Palaces were always packed with ladies, so it is no wonder that intrigue among them was vicious, if undercover. They vied and fought to see whose son would be named crown prince and who could manage the ruler most adroitly.

It was a woman, Herodotus says, who persuaded Darius to make war on Greece. And she had been persuaded in her turn by a Greek physician trapped in Darius's golden cage (for that is what life in the Persian court was) and longing for home. If war with Greece were imminent, the doctor thought, perhaps Darius might think to use his services as a spy. Once across the Mediterranean, he could break free. Things turned out exactly as the doctor had planned.

Darius did make his war and was wholly unsuccessful in it (as we shall relate in another chapter). Xerxes, his son, thinking to recoup his father's lost prestige, assembled the largest and most motley army yet seen in the Old World. He, too, was unsuccessful. Persian armies retreated over the Hellespont, and Persian kings confined themselves thereafter to dabbling unobtrusively in Greek politics and influencing events abroad with threats and bribes. They also made use of Greek mercenaries in their own military machine. Never again, however, would they come back in person to Greece. Greece came, instead, to them. Xerxes had once said that Persia must defeat the Greeks or be defeated by them. And so it turned out.

Anatolia, particularly coastal Anatolia, had always been troublesome to the Persians, and it was to be Anatolia that triggered the Achaemenid downfall. There were Greek cities all along the coast, forever restive under Persian rule. It was to "liberate" these cities that Macedonian Alexander in 334 B.C. crossed into Anatolia, conquered there, and moved on to set up a Hellenistic empire where a Persian one had been.

The Hellenistic interlude lasted little over a hundred years and left few marks behind. True, there was a general stepping up of trade with the Far East, with China, the silk empire. Trade was something Greek colonists understood profoundly. But by this time Persia had already achieved her own distinct form of civilization and she resisted change.

In 248 B.C. parts of the empire began to revolt against their Hellenized rulers. By the end of that century most of Persia was once again in native hands, and Persians were treated to a revival of old-fashioned Iranian customs. City life had never been terribly popular with true Persians as it was with the Greeks and the Mesopotamians. It was to be less popular still.

The authors of this swing to the past were members of the Arsacid family of Parthia, a Persian province. They were of Scythian descent and, living as they did far out into the steppes, were unsoftened by the luxuries of Mesopotamia and Greece. It had been no trouble at all for them to oust the Hellenistic masters of Persia and rule the empire on their own account. The Romans, newly come at about this time to their own ascendancy, found the Parthians formidable enemies. Several Roman armies were defeated on Persian soil, their soldiers carted off to far stretches of the steppe. Parthian horsemanship was proverbial among the Romans. So was Parthian government, a system of feudalism which even in Roman terms was considered harsh and autocratic.

If Parthia was harsh in government, chaining her people to their land and occupations, she was quite tolerant about religious expression. Anybody in Parthian lands was free to believe and worship as he chose. The Arsacids themselves, being followers of archaic Iranian forms, preferred Mithra to Ahuramazda and skipped altogether the complex teachings of Zoroaster.

Perhaps it was during late Parthian times, in the second century A.D., that a garbled form of the old Iranian religion developed in Persian Anatolia and crept from there into Rome. Anatolian tribute troops, exacted by Rome in some military struggle or other, took their beliefs with them. The new religion, called Mithraism, spread like wildfire wherever Roman soldiers traveled, for it was a soldier's religion, a military religion, and no wonder. Mithraism emphasized on a spiritual plane what warriors knew best in the everyday: battle. Zoroaster's Evil Spirit was no longer subject to the Lord of Light but had become an evil god in his own right. And the Great One himself (no longer called Ahuramazda) was thought to have withdrawn, to be remote, unconcerned with earthly affairs. The whole burden of battle was born by Mithras, golden Mithras, Lord of the Sun, savior of man. It was up to good soldiers to fight alongside this golden general, and soldiers did.

The rites of Mithraism were simple, though bloody, involving the sacrifice of a bull (a thing strictly forbidden by Zoroaster). There were no theological discussions, no hymns, and not even very many prayers. Religious writings left behind by these soldiers of Mithras are plain, downright announcements that someone had been initiated into such-and-such a rank. Hail!

Initiates of Mithras moved upward through the ranks of holiness just as they progressed upward through military ranks. There were seven ranks corresponding to the five known planets and the sun and moon, dangerous spheres the worshiper would have to pass after death on his way toward Seventh Heaven. An obsession with planets, stars, and astrology came with Mithraism into Rome. Because of this obsession, the days of the Roman week changed from nine to seven, and each was named for a planet and the god in charge of it. Naturally, in deference to Mithraism, the holy day was the first day, the day dedicated to the sun. And to this day, Sunday begins the week for many people in the Western world. To the soldiers of Mithras, no day was more sacred than December 25, for on that day (so they believed) the Sun Lord had been born, brought forth by a lightning bolt from the prison of a mighty rock. (December 25 is still special in the Christian world and still because of a savior's birth.)

After 225 A.D. or so the Parthian Arsacids were overthrown by their own vassals, a clan from old Pars—true descendants, they said, of the Achaemenid royal line. The new rulers (Sassanids by name) fervently championed Zoroastrian doctrine, using it and the influence of the Magi to bolster their own shaky claims to the throne. It was they who saw to it that Zoroastrian doctrines—most of them preserved only in the memories of devotees—were at last collected and put into writing. Soon Persia became as strict and orthodox in religious observances as it was in terms of political life. A man prayed and believed and learned in ways that were thought appropriate to his position in life. And he attained his position in life by being born into it. His birth alone destined him to riches or poverty, helplessness or power. It was nearly impossible for a man to rise in importance by his own efforts or initiative. All were fixed on an ascending scale of worth which ended in the person of the emperor.

Things came to be much the same in the Eastern Roman Empire, in Byzantium, Persia's neighbor in Anatolia. For a thousand years Persia had been opponent and almost alter ego to the west (much as Russia and America are to one another today). It had been the Achaemenids versus Greece; the Parthians versus Rome; and from the third to the seventh centuries A.D., it was to be Sassanian Persia versus Byzantium. For a thousand years the two worlds warred, and in warring, they learned well one another's tricks and ways. They had borrowed ideas from one another (though in later days and on Middle Eastern soil, Rome did most of the borrowing). It is thanks to Persia that we have such exotic words as *bazaar, jasmine, magic, turban, azure*—even *pajama*—and such games as polo (designed for gentlemen who lived as much on horseback as on their own feet) and chess (*checkmate* comes from *shah mat,* the king is dead).

For a thousand years Persia and her antagonists to the west welcomed one another's refugees—first the political malcontents, then the out-of-favor intellectuals, then the religious heretics. For a thousand years they traded back and forth the same disputed parcels of land, influenced one another's politics, and supported one another's favorite rulers. By 500 A.D. they (along with faraway China) were the last islands of civilization in a barbarian world. But not for long.

In 640 A.D. men of Arabia—desert-bred, desert-hard, and armed with a potent new religion—swept all before them, conquering the Middle East to the very gates of Constantinople. Most of Persia was converted to Islam. Die-hard Zoroastrians fled to India, where they are known today as the Parsees. The Persian language incorporated many Arab words and tones. And Persian culture (itself now the sophisticated teacher to the barbarian intruder) adjusted and altered once again toward still another meeting of minds.

Of barbarians among city folk, the story is everywhere and at all times the same: they come to plunder and they stay to be tamed—to be tamed, to be merged, to be forgotten. Of all the Indo-European Battle-ax People and their kin, the Persians, who came last into the Middle Eastern world, stayed the longest and with the most success. But even they changed that world less than they were changed by it.

In Europe, events took a different turn. The earliest of the incoming nomads encountered few folk beyond their own level of development. Cities were distant and from them ideas came slowly and in manageable doses. There was time to receive and to adjust old ways to suit changing situations. And in time something quite new began.

Part II

MOVING WEST

7. Minoans and Mycenaeans

Something New in Europe

There is a land named Crete, fruitful and fair,
Set like a jewel in the wine-dark sea,
Peopled by countless multitudes of men
And ninety cities . . .

So Homer sang of the island from which civilization skipped to Europe. When he sang, the cities of Crete had already crumbled and their multitudes had flown. But although he never saw it, Homer sang truly of Crete, where the Minoans (called thus for Minos, the name of their kings) built great gleaming cities—unwalled cities, for sturdy ships and the wide sea itself were Crete's defense. Chief among Cretan cities was Knossos, built around a royal palace called the Labyrinth, a word meaning "the house of the ax"—the double ax, which had, for Cretans, a religious significance. The palace was a

marvel of columned walks and flights of graceful stairs. There was such a bewildering maze of rooms and corridors that the half-barbarous Greeks who saw it thought of the Labyrinth as a terrifying puzzle—something like a carnival fun house in which a man could be lost forever. It is with the meaning "maze"—and an underground maze at that—that the word appears in Greek legends about Crete. And this is what *labyrinth* means to us still.

Cretan land was fair but not everywhere well watered, so the Cretans were driven—perhaps by need, perhaps by inclination—to the sea. Around 2000 B.C., when their name first appears in the records of other ancient peoples (the Egyptians called them Keftiu), they are already merchants. Eventually they came to exercise a sort of rule over the Aegean hinterlands beyond their trading posts, offering both protection and manufactured goods in return for tribute and raw materials.

The Cretans, however, were not empire builders in the way of the great landed nations. They never exercised power or even influence in the Middle East. Perhaps that is one reason they were so quickly forgotten, supplanted by the aggressive, ambitious early Greeks, who found it natural to take power where they found it.

The Cretan empire was the sea, and it occupied all the thinking of these people. Creatures from the sea appeared as decorations on everything—from palace walls to wine jars. Recognizing the importance of attractive packaging, the Cretans sold their olive oil and wine in jugs and jars that would be treasured long after the original contents had disappeared. Nobody knows just how much of the Mediterranean was known to Cretan sailors. All of it, very likely, to and through the Pillars of Hercules (what we call now the Straits of Gibraltar). They may even have made landfall in England—herself one distant day to be an island empire.

It seems nearly certain that the Cretans came originally from Anatolia. Their religious life, their pottery styles, house types, and burials all reflect Neolithic influences from that source. It is beginning to seem possible (at least, to some scholars) that Anatolian traditions were reinforced in Crete, not by a second wave of Anatolian natives, but by the Battle-ax Luwians whom we met in Chapter 3. Sometime around 2200 B.C., you will recall, fire and destruction were carried over parts of western Anatolia by an intrusive people thought to have been the Luwians. This same sort of havoc occurred at about the same time in Greece—probably also at the hands of Luwians, though some scholars blame the disaster on invaders who would one day be Greeks. Whoever caused the fires, Luwians did appear in the Aegean. They must have come early, because there are in Greece and in Crete as well a host of place names and plant names which are not Greek but which can be linked to similar sorts of names in western and southern Anatolia where Luwians are known to have settled. These are names with *-ssos* endings—Knossos, Halicarnassos (a city in Anatolia), Parnassos (a Greek mountain with an ancient shrine). The word *parnassos* (which means "a shrine") has turned up in several of the languages in which Hittite documents were kept. Words with *-nthos* endings—*labyrinth(os)*, *hyacinth(os)*, *korinthos* (Corinth, a city in Greece)—are also thought to be Luwian in origin.

The Luwians seem to have treated Crete with respect. There was no burning, no havoc on the island. Whether they lacked boats or simply missed getting to the island until after their warlike fires had cooled, no one can say. Their words made their way across the waters, however, and at some point so did they. Through the years the Luwians maintained their Anatolian connections, so that developments there and on the island kept even pace. The strikingly beautiful palace ruins of Crete (the final phases were built around 1700 B.C.), the shrines, and the ornaments are in many ways similar to ruins in coastal Anatolia and belong, as well, in the same time slot.

Three systems of writing developed in Crete. Earliest was a pictographic—or as some call it, a hieroglyphic—system. The other two (which we know as Linear A and Linear B) contain similar syllable signs, used for two different spoken languages. Only Linear B, the latest in terms of time, has been fully deciphered. It was used to write the archaic Greek dialect spoken by the Achaeans—Battle-ax People who moved down into the peninsula some time after the Luwian arrival and rose to dominance there and, later, in Crete. The whole of the subject matter (at least in Linear B tablets so far discovered) involves inventory—lists of goods, weapons, and chariots in palace armories, and lists of offerings in temple stores.

Philologist Leonard Palmer believes that the older syllabary, Linear A, was invented to record Luwian words. If this proves to be so, what language do the hieroglyphs represent? Luwian also? Some forgotten

The Minoan-Mycenaean World

Anatolian tongue, already ancient when herders speaking an Indo-European language appeared on the scene? No one knows, and the cautious scholar would not hazard a guess. But how very appropriate such an outcome would be! Cretan writings would then represent the three strains of culture—old Anatolian, Battle-ax Luwian, and Battle-ax Achaean—which, in mingling, produced on that jeweled island something wholly new.

If Babylon was the London of the ancient world, Knossos of Crete was certainly Paris. A painting of one young lady, in fact, has been dubbed "La Parisienne" by the archaeologist who discovered her. And no wonder. There is about her, about her people, a lighthearted gaiety, a grace, a sense of fun and spontaneity utterly foreign to the older peoples of the world—conscious of their age and overgrown with pretensions. The Minoans, seemingly, were not bound by rigid conventions. They were not warlike, forever boasting of armies conquered and captives slain. Neither grave paintings nor grave goods contain a hint of weaponry. Cretan art dwells rather on animals and flowers, the out-of-doors, and, of course, on the people themselves. They were proud (to the point of vanity) of their handsome, smiling faces and their wasp waists, and men as well as women strove to enhance their good looks in every possible way. Nowhere else could one find such a sense of style in clothing. Women dressed coquettishly in long, tiered skirts, high heels, floppy hats, and certainly they had the utmost in plunging necklines. Men wore brief trunks and ornamental daggers. And both men and women admired curly ringlets adorned with jewelry and/or flowers.

Everyone seems to have been tolerably well off in sunny Crete. Even slavery was at a minimum. Cretan houses were airy, light, tasteful. Their owners obviously cherished comfort and convenience, for they installed bathrooms complete with flushing plumbing.

The worship of the Great Earth Mother—portrayed sometimes with snakes, sometimes with other animals, sometimes (as in Anatolia) with a young spouse, symbol of the ever-recurring cycles of death and life—took place not in vast temples but in caves or out of doors under the sky. There solemn dance pageants were held and harvest processions of great joy.

The ceremonial double ax (Luwian influence, perhaps?) was a sign sacred to the Mother. So were the horns of the bull. The "horns of consecration," they are called. The bull itself was a sacred animal (as indeed it had been in Anatolia) and figured often as an art motif. This part of the Mediterranean lives at the mercy of the earthquake, which hereabouts, if one listens closely, sounds for all the world like a great angry bull bellowing and pawing the ground. Perhaps this is one reason why the bull was revered, the great sea bull whose attributes Greek Poseidon would later take to himself. Perhaps this is one reason why the Cretans celebrated in their palace arenas a spectacle part sport, part dance, part ceremony—a spectacle which may indeed have been the starting point of the bullfight, still the national sport of Spain. In the Cretan spectacle, boy and girl acrobats somersaulted between the horns and over the backs of charging bulls. Behind the bull stood a partner waiting to catch and steady the vaulting dancer and help him elude the enraged animal. It was a game which took skill and nerve as well as endless, grueling training. The casualty rates must have been high. Cretan aristocrats, the first performers in this deadly game (or ritual or sacrifice), eventually must have turned it over to professionals in much the same way that the Spanish gentlemen abdicated their rights in the bullring in favor of professional matadors. When Cretan professionals dwindled in number, entrepreneurs may have taken to importing the barbarian youngsters of the mainland. Perhaps "demanding" is a better word, or even "stealing."

Here is where the Greek legends come to life. Remember the story

of Theseus? His father, the Athenian king, had yearly to surrender to the Cretan suzerain a quota of youths and maidens. According to the legend, the young people were to be fodder for a monster, half man, half bull. His name itself makes the picture clear: Minotauros—the Bull of Minos. Perhaps it was to dance before Minos's bull in the sacred arena of the Labyrinth that the youths were taken, and not, as the legend has it, to be eaten in the monster's underground maze. Either way the end results were likely much the same. It is possible, too, that the officiating priest at the arena ceremonies may have worn a bull's mask over his own head, helping thus to set off rumors of the terrible Minotaur.

The legend tells still more. Theseus escaped and took his companions home again, along with a Cretan princess whose love and help he had won. Having noted the weaknesses of Cretan defenses, Theseus, it is said, gathered ships from other mainland cities and descended on

Knossos. In the midst of a dreadful earthquake, he toppled mighty Minos and a mainland dynasty began to rule in Crete. Other legends hold that Theseus came to his kingdom, not through violence, but because of his marriage to the Cretan heiress.

Archaeology adds substance to the legend if not to the figure of Theseus himself. If he existed at all, he must have been a princely descendant of one group of Battle-ax People who had, sometime before 1600 B.C., moved down from the northern steppes into the Aegean region. These early Greek-speaking people—Achaeans, Homer called them, or Mycenaeans, after the name of their chief mainland stronghold—filtered and sometimes burned their way among farmers in possession of the mainland. These native people were largely wedded to Cretan ways and worshiped the Cretan goddess. Perhaps they and the Cretans as well reckoned descent through the mother's side of the family. Certainly it is true that women were important in this part of the world. Much more than they would be after the Achaeans took hold in the land. And much, *much* more than they would be in classical Greek times. The patriarchal, warrior Achaeans and their male, warrior gods married native girls and native goddesses, and some rather different social forms emerged. The old ways of behaving and believing were not altogether subdued on the mainland, but they did undergo some transformation with the nuptials, as Linear B writings of later times let us know.

Many Linear B tablets mention the names of Achaean (later to be classical Greek) gods—Zeus, Enyalios (Ares), Poseidon, Hermes, Paiawon (Apollo). On these tablets—all records of offerings from pious believers—the great goddess is by no means slighted. She is addressed variously as Atana (Athena, already patroness of Athens?), as Hera, as Eleuthia (protectress of childbirth), as Potnia, which means simply "Our Lady," or as Wanassa (King-ess). There is even one title which points directly toward the source of the culture influences which tamed and harnessed the Achaean invaders. It is "Our Lady of the Labyrinth."

From their first arrival on the Greek mainland—probably, as we have noted, sometime before 1600 B.C.—the Achaeans seem to have absorbed all they could of Cretan arts and graces. Their grave goods tell us so. They adopted Cretan dress, bought Cretan goods, and affected Cretan manners. But somehow they could never assume the Cretan outlook on life. They were decidedly aggressive where the Cretans were gentle, patriarchally clannish where the Cretans were urbanized and urbane. They preferred hunting lions and wild boars to Cretan festivals of dance and song, and they had Cretan artists put just such hunting scenes on golden daggers, silver cups, and every other useful item.

Most of all, Achaeans liked to fight. Finding that this sport could be successfully pursued afloat, they became sailors, hunters, and raiders of the sea. In short, pirates. They grew rich in piracy, richer still in trade, until at last they quite put the Cretan mercantile nose out of joint. To the high-walled Mycenaean fortresses—so different in character from the open, airy Cretan cities—there came increasing numbers of merchants from abroad. In Mycenaean harbors the ships grew in number along with the warriors to man them. And one day the Cretan rulers were overturned by the ruled; one day a Greek-speaking suzerain gave justice in Knossos. Greek-speaking, certainly, for it was during this crucial time, this time of change and transition, that the Linear A syllabary was used for writing Greek—the form we know as Linear B. Clay tablets found in Knossos and dated at around 1400 B.C. let us know approximately when the shift took place.

However the Greeks came to power in Crete—whether through wealth, through dynastic marriage, or through war—the Theseus legend somehow captures the event. Not with total accuracy, to be sure. Legends have little regard for time or sequence of events. Always, however, there is a kernel of truth. And when legends can be used to shed light on archaeological discoveries, always a clearer picture of the distant past comes swimming into focus.

Greek rulers of Crete did not succeed to mastery of the Aegean but probably simply deputized for the high king in Mycenae. For the Achaeans during this period of their history seem to have been more tightly knit, more united than Greeks would be for another thousand years—until Alexander's time.

Released from Cretan restraint, the Achaeans took up the reins of trade and exploration with undisguised zest, carrying the now combined Minoan-Mycenaean culture to ever more distant shores. The export-import business with Egypt continued without a break. Mycenaean art objects were as much a fad with wealthy Egyptians as ever the Cretan wares had been. The Egyptians scarcely noticed that a different people now manned the "Keftiu" trading post on the Delta.

"Mycenae, rich in gold," is how Homer described the Achaeans' chief city. We cannot doubt him. Achaean burials—first in shaft graves made and furnished according to the old Battle-ax pattern, then in elaborate tholos tombs made in imitation of Cretan models—have revealed wealth beyond dreaming. Some may represent return for Egyptian trade, some may be payment to Achaean mercenaries for military help in Egyptian campaigns. It is even possible that Hyksos princes, driven out of Egypt about 1550 B.C., took refuge among the distantly related Achaeans. (The Greek myth of Danaüs records just such an event.) Perhaps this explains why Egyptian objects appear in Mycenaean tombs and why certain unusual customs were introduced —the modeling of gold-foil masks over the bearded faces of dead chieftains, for example. We do not know who brought horses and chariots to Greece—refugee Hyksos or the Achaeans themselves. Perhaps horses had arrived earlier with the Luwians. In any case, it was

between 1600 and 1500 B.C. that carvings of horses and chariots began
to be placed in Achaean graves.

The Achaeans may have learned trading from the Cretans, but they
never lost their fondness for raids, for grabbing cattle and booty and
land, too, where it was available. Hittite records suggest that Achaeans
held some parts of coastal Anatolia. Miletus seems to have been one of
their Anatolian possessions, a city destined to be the birthplace of
new thought in later, sadder times.

It was against a vassal of the Hittite Empire that Mycenae chose to
pit her growing might. And it was because of this conflict that (thanks to
Homer) the Achaeans were to be remembered. The conflict took
place at Troy, probably sometime around 1250 B.C.

Did it start, romantically, because of beautiful Helen? Or was it
because of a prosaic trade rivalry, because Mycenae wanted to break
through Troy's blockade to the rich towns lining the Black Sea?
(The tale of the Argonauts doggedly seeking the Golden Fleece suggests this longing.) Perhaps, after all, the real cause was a combina-
tion of the romantic and the practical—and maybe one or two other
considerations into the bargain. Few events have simple beginnings—
wars least of all.

For a long time the wonderful *Iliad* and *Odyssey,* which gave that
little war immortality, were thought to be fiction pure and simple.
One man, Heinrich Schliemann, believed them to be sober fact—had
believed this ever since he had first read them as a boy. And he set
out to prove his convictions. In 1870, digging in a little mound just
where the legends directed, he found Troy. Not one, but many Troys,
one on top of another, in layer-cake fashion. Included was Homer's
Troy, the burned and sacked Troy of the legend, though it was somehow missed by the excavator the first time around. Skipping then to
Greece, Schliemann uncovered Mycenae and thus gave real credentials

to the vanished Achaeans. Sir Arthur Evans, digging subsequently in Crete, found the Minoan civilization, the extent of which, the importance of which even Homer himself could hardly have known.

Homer's epics were not committed to paper until around 800 B.C.—long, long after the events they immortalized—the battles of Achaeans and Trojans, the wrath of Achilles, the wanderings of Odysseus. And whether the epics were the work of one genius or of many contributing bards no one can say for sure. In any case, they mix fantasy and fact, elements from Mycenaean times and elements from later Greek times. The two-horse chariot (later Greeks used four), bronze weapons (later Greeks used iron), tower shields (Greeks preferred round ones) —all these are pure Mycenaean, as are the funeral games and the general slaughter of men and animals in honor of the dead Patroclus. But his cremation is strictly later Greek (the Achaeans entombed their dead). One suspects that the Greek warriors of those last, glowing years of Minoan-Mycenaean culture must have been just a bit more sophisticated, more civilized than Homer's rowdy heroes.

Everyone knows how the Greeks won by the use of guile. (We're still prone to describing traps and ruses as Trojan horses.) Everyone knows about the trials of Odysseus. (Writers still call any long wandering search an odyssey.) Homer sang well of the Achaean triumph. It was a triumph all too brief, all too short-lived.

Barely forty years after the Achaean ships sailed home, sometime around 1200 B.C., the Dorians came, and a dark age descended over the Aegean. Perhaps it was not truly so dark as it is most often thought to have been. The Dorians, another Battle-ax group, were, after all, northern cousins of the Achaeans, Greek-speaking (though with a somewhat different dialect), and so, able in some measure to appreciate Mycenaean achievements. But this did not prevent them from destroying the Mycenaean cities of the mainland and the Minoan-Mycenaean cities of Crete. Clay tablets found in Pylos—those terse business records baked hard in the fires of battle—bear mute witness to the preparations made for the expected invasion: the stores of chariot wheels, the command units mustered, the ships' crews summoned, the coast watchers posted to give warning of attack.

Neither did the bonds of language prevent the Dorians from breaking up the unified Mycenaean community into small, manageable units. In time, neighbors just over the next mountain would be strangers to each other. Scribes, court personnel, and men of rank and learning fled the country or were slain. Some refugees sailed to the Syrian coast. Others settled along the Ionian Coast in Anatolia. There they kept alive the combined cultures of Crete and Mycenae, intact, ready to hand for another day.

With the refugees, all knowledge of writing departed Hellenic shores. It was not until the Phoenicians—another sea people of the Syrian coast—brought the Semitic alphabet to Greece that records could once again be kept and Homer's stories of a time long past preserved for the world.

The Dorians were not everywhere supreme. They never quite overcame Athens and its surrounding hamlets, nor Boeotia, nor the Cyclades, nor even mountainous Arcadia. But Crete and especially the Peloponnese were bent to Dorian will. Sparta—the ultimate military state of later Greek times—would be a direct product of Dorian design.

In time, however, even the lubberly conquerors took to the sea, moved out into the islands, began to trade. In time they, too, were moved by the golden wealth of the past—the free, gay spirit of Crete, the ambitious curiosity of Mycenae. In time their common zest for venturing, for daring the unknown and unknowable, would fire not only explorers of the sea but explorers of ideas as well—not only mariners, but scientists and philosophers and dreamers of dreams. And in time came the golden flowering of Greece.

8. Golden Greece

The Flowering

. . . Ours is a constitution which does not imitate those of our neighbors, but is rather a pattern to others. Because power rests with the majority and not with a few, it is called a democracy; in private disputes all are equal before the law, and in public life men are honored for conspicuous achievement in any act, and not for sectional reasons; nor is any poor man, who has it in him to do good service to the city, prevented by his obscurity. Ours is a free state, both in politics and in daily life. . . .

That speech—with its mixture of truth and pride and exaggeration—could have been made yesterday at any political rally. It could have been made in America or in England or in almost any capital of the Western world. It was not. Pericles of Athens delivered that speech nearly twenty-five hundred years ago. If listeners today can warm

to his words, politicians today would have felt thoroughly at home among the voters to whom he spoke. And no wonder. Nearly everything in our political life has been modeled after Greek originals. (The very words *politics* and *democracy* come from Greek roots.) If our actual machinery of government owes a bit more to the practical Romans, still the ideal behind it is Greek. For the notion that men are capable of ruling themselves—quite independently of kings and priests—and that man's reason can be a proper guide in human affairs began in Greece. The personality of the politician was molded there. So were the rhetoric of political speeches and the mechanics of political debate. And so was the unpredictable personality of the ordinary voter, who (then as now) sometimes threw the "ins" out just because he was tired of seeing their faces.

It is not Greek politics alone which ring familiarly in our twentieth-century ears. We can scarcely read anything written in those days without having queer twinges of recognition, without wanting to say, "I saw that in the paper, just yesterday!" Colorful personalities of that antique world stand out just as sharply as if they were in today's newsprint—big as life and twice as ornery. So do the courtroom trials and arguments and decisions, both wise and stupid.

Science means much to us, and we value our achievements in this realm. Yet the Greeks beat us to nearly every major scientific theory —and beat us by two and a half millennia. Democritus proposed the first atomic theory, Anaximander, the first theory of evolution, and Aristarchus, the first theory that the earth orbits the sun, not the other way around. This notion, when rediscovered in Renaissance times by Copernicus, caused a religious upheaval, a storm of learned controversy, and goodness knows how many public trials and executions. In the older Greek world, hinged as it was on reason and the rational man, it stirred only a ripple of interest. Another theory? Fine. Every philosopher had theories. Wasn't that what philosophers were for?

. . . I will prescribe regimen for the good of my patients according to my ability and my judgment and never do harm to anyone. . . . I will preserve the purity of my life and my art. . . . All that may come to my knowledge in the exercise of my profession or in daily commerce with men, which ought not to be spread abroad, I will keep secret and never reveal. . . .

That is part of an oath written by a great physician long ago in Greece. It was taken by his students as they entered medical practice. It is still taken by physicians today. Besides stating so aptly the physician's trust, Hippocrates was the first physician to keep accurate records of his patients' progress in their diseases. And he diagnosed on the basis of his observations without reference to magic or superstition or the supernatural.

Greek plays are still presented on our stages. The comedies are full of "modern" jokes. The tragedies move today's audiences as deeply as they did when first performed. All our theatrical words come from Greek words—*comedy* and *tragedy, orchestra, proscenium, drama, scene*. Actors are often called thespians after Thespis, the dramatist who created for himself the first starring role. (It caused a scandal in his time.) All he did was to move apart from the chorus (another word derived from the Greek) and speak his own lines solo (still another word of Greek origin).

Greek sculpture and Greek painting, rediscovered in Renaissance times, dominated ideals of art for centuries. And Greek temples, with their lovely columns, their symmetry, and their grace, have long been the models for public buildings and monuments all over the Western world. Everywhere they are glorified versions of the hall-and-porch known and used throughout Anatolia and the steppes for huts and burial chambers. It was Greek genius that transformed this simple plan into a temple.

Any modern study of philosophy begins with the Greek philosophers, who said it all and said it best. But the Greeks were not concerned solely with philosophy's humanistic view of life and the pursuit of reason. They were concerned with feeling, too, religious feeling, and mystic rites, which echo still in many a churchly ceremony today. In classic times, the worship of the Olympian gods was mostly a worship of the personified city-state, which was, to the Greek, his real center of pride and belonging. Rural folk gave their devotion to nature spirits left over from ancient times. But under all was The Mother, the old earth mother of Anatolia and Crete and Mycenae, whose worship re-emerged in the Eleusinian rites honoring corn-goddess Demeter and the daughter stolen from her and at last restored. Eleusis was near Athens, and the rites came to be part of Athenian city life, thus binding together old ways and new. But these rites were different, even so, from the regular city celebrations. They were secret, not public, and their concentration was on the life hereafter rather than the city here on earth. The initiate (and only he) was to know bliss beyond the grave. Said Sophocles, the playwright:

> Thrice happy are those of mortals who, having seen those rites, depart for Hades; for to them alone is it granted to have true life there; to the rest all there is evil.

Greek poetry long ago set the style in literature for the Western world. Poets enjoyed special honor in ancient times. It was to them that the Greeks turned for revelation of the beauty and mystery of life. In their songs, the myths and legends of the Olympian gods (mingled with the even more ancient religious ideas of Crete and Mycenae) became dominant themes—themes which we are still repeating today. Sorrowing Demeter, wise and valiant Athena, remorseful Oedipus, vengeful Electra. Some of these themes have been treated on our stages in plays performed in modern dress. Some have given names to scientific concepts. They live on, those old gods and heroes. They simply will not die.

The Olympic Games were begun (as we learn and learn again every four years) in Greece. And the records kept of them help us to construct the first really accurate catalogues of ancient history. The Greeks loved sports almost as much as they loved talking, and winning athletes were honored almost as highly as famous poets. Wrestling and boxing, track and field sports—discus throwing, javelin hurling, sprints and relays—all these began you know where and with you know whom. At our modern athletic meets, it is not just the list of events which harks back to Hellenic games. The whole protocol, the emphasis on sportsmanship and form, the attention to the ancient rules and rites, all of it maintains a tradition as valid now as then.

So much of our heritage is richly Greek that it is hard to believe in what a short time that heritage was forged. It is hard to credit such an impact to such a brief golden age, an age that lasted little more than fifty years. Creative as the Greeks were, they could also destroy. And after their short, hectic blooming, they destroyed themselves.

The Greeks were paradoxical, a study in contradictions. Though their scientific theorizing was brilliant, novel, and daring, most could not, would not experiment for proof. And so their great leaps of imagination, of intuition, went only so far and no further. They never thought of testing, because very often that would have involved sweaty hand labor. And work with the hands (except for writing, of course) was considered to be beneath a proper gentleman. Athletics were something else again. Games were fun. And mental exercise should be fun, too. Logic, reasoning, speculation, they thought, should be toys of the mind. Reduced to practical levels, tested, and worried, ideas lost their purity and became work. Work—hard work, uninteresting work—was for slaves. It was all they were good for. Or so Greek thinking ran.

Just there lay a second contradiction. These people who spoke so eloquently of the dignity of human life, the value of reason, and the worth of the individual would not apply these ideals to people who, being slaves, were therefore considered somehow less than human. Spectators who could weep during a tragedy depicting Trojan women at the mercy of their conquerors could themselves sack cities and sell citizens into slavery without a qualm.

Women, too, in these stimulating times of art and learning were merely onlookers, not participants. And not even onlookers much of the time. Good women were confined to their houses, for the most part, there to sew and weave, superintend the slaves and their own daughters. (Boys were removed at the age of seven from their mothers' care.) Wives did not eat with their husbands or converse with them or attend dinner parties in their company. (Parties were, in any case, all "stag.") Poor faceless drabs, how could they be interesting companions, uneducated as they were kept? Women of unquenchable talent and ability *could* sometimes mingle with brilliant men, attend lectures, and learn from philosophers. But the price they paid for this freedom was their reputation and the privilege of honorable marriage. It was a hard choice to make.

"The Greeks were not meant to give rest to themselves or anybody else," said Thucydides, historian of the Peloponnesian War. And so it seems. For all their talk of the Golden Mean, of stern civic duty, and calm philosophy, the Greeks were seldom able to practice what they preached. They were forever spoiling their best intentions with hot tempers, passion, and pride. To think of the Greeks is to think, right away, of a beautiful, pure-white temple perched majestically on a hill. One forgets that in their prime all those temples were gaudily painted. So were the statues and the friezes. All of them.

Time has worn the colors away and left only the pure marble behind. Just as time has obscured Greek passions and frailties and kept for us only the nobility of their words.

It is in politics—the chief pride of the creative Greeks—that the paradox stands out most vividly. Their whole achievement was in independent city government. It never went beyond the city. That sense of civic identity which we saw beginning with the Sumerians came to its finest flower with the Greeks—and went no further. Athens, under Pericles, did dream of a larger unity, but only as an extension of Athenian pride and Athenian ways.

Greece was not just a tale of two cities as many people would like to think—of Athens: creative, excessive, brawling, and brilliant, Mycenaean in heritage, versus Sparta: totalitarian, uncreative, brave, and rigid, Dorian in heritage. It is a tale of a hundred cities—spread not just along the Greek coast line, but all around the Mediterranean and

Greek Settlements in the Seventh Century B.C.
•Location of cities

the Black Sea as well. They shared—all these cities—in a common culture, a common reverence for poetry and beauty, a common enthusiasm for sports. And once every year or so they met in peaceful competition at the Olympic Games. At this time sacred truces were honored. Greek cities, however, shared no common laws, no system of connecting roads, no binding links, no concerted action. Ancient ties between cities, the fabric of a common way of life had been cut by the Dorians after 1200 B.C., cut so thoroughly that no patching was possible. Now and then cities formed temporary and uneasy leagues. But for the most part each city clung jealously to its own ways, its own citizens, and plague take the others!

It was in this separatism—sparked by the fires of successive foreign invasions, heightened in the competition of much-mixed and adventurous people—that the rich heritage of classical Greece came into being. For a look at beginnings, we shall have to backtrack again and pick up the story where we left off at the end of Chapter 7.

The Dorian dark age began to lift, perhaps around 900 B.C. Writing returned—a gift of the Phoenicians. Trade was resumed, colonists sent out again. Cities took shape or were reformed on the ashes of Dorian destruction and in memory of things past. Each experimented with different political machinery. Athens suffered from demagogues, class wars, and bankruptcy until the redoubtable Solon (our legislators are still sometimes called solons) persuaded the citizens to accept a new constitution and a measure of stability. This was sometime around 594 B.C. Some cities, Corinth for one, threw out their Dorian dynasts and tried self-government. Sparta, however, brought down once and for all its iron curtain, behind which it promoted rigid eugenics (only the fit might breed; only fit offspring survived), absolute discipline, and that utter devotion to the state which was to make of it the most feared military power of its time. The natives of ancient Mycenaean and Cretan stock were utterly subjugated, bound to the soil, and occasionally hunted down as a means of ensuring docility.

In the midst of all this internal concentration, things were happening abroad which would turn Greece about-face once again. Around 560 B.C. old Mycenaean cities along the Anatolian coast were threatened with engulfment first by King Croesus, ruler of an Anatolian kingdom called Lydia (where descendants of ancient Luwians still lived), then by Persian Cyrus. The Ionians replied by fielding armies against their would-be masters. What is more, they sent home to the mainland for help. Athens and other Greek cities dispatched ships and men, who were soundly defeated along with the city armies they had been sent to rescue. In 494 B.C., a horde of refugees streamed back home again.

With them they brought all the treasured learning from the old pre-Dorian days plus the stores of scientific lore from Babylon, the wonder stories of Egypt, the sea knowledge of Syria. It was from all the bits and pieces, from this mongrel treasure, that Greek thought took wing.

Conquering Anatolia and sending refugees streaming home was not enough for the Persians. You will recall how Darius I, successor to Cyrus, considered himself affronted by the arrogance of those nasty little Greek cities across the Hellespont and how, to salve his injured dignity, he resolved to add all of Hellas to the Persian Empire by a grand invasion.

Cities along the line of march fell or treated with the invaders. Last to bar the way was Athens. To her assistance came only the little town of Plataea. The other cities hedged and temporized. When at last their soldiers arrived, it was all over but the shouting, and the Athenians had won the battle of Marathon all by themselves.

It was not that the Persians lacked numbers. They were greater

in manpower several times over the Athenians. It was not that they
lacked bravery, either. They were, it is true, a motley array, wearing
many costumes, speaking many tongues—Scythian, Assyrian, Arabian.
Herodotus says there were even Ethiopian bowmen in the line of
march. They were unused to disciplined battle, they were unused
to one another, and the Athenian solid phalanx, bristling with spears
and moving as one man, must have been to them an awesome sight.
Most of all, the Persian army faced free men fighting for their own
homes, their own city, and themselves as part of that city. And that
must have been awesome, too. It was summed up by Herodotus in his
report of a conversation which took place between Greek and Persian
gentlemen. The Greek said to the Persian:

> Freedom you have never tried, to know
> how sweet it is. If you had, you would urge
> us to fight for it not with our spears only,
> but even with hatchets.

The Battle of Marathon was won in 490 B.C. Ten years later the
Persians came again with an even bigger army and a tremendous
fleet of ships. Xerxes, son of Darius, built a bridge of boats across the
Hellespont for the transport of his men, equipment, and horses. This
time, at last, the Greek cities did manage to cooperate (all except for
Thebes). A small contingent of Spartans, led by their king, Leonidas,
held the Persian hordes at the pass of Thermopylae. With this delay
they bought time in which Greece could prepare. Of the Spartans
who fought that day, only two men remained to take back word of
the slaughter. One later hanged himself for shame; the other died in
the Battle of Plataea.

This time the Persians won through to Athens and burned down
the city. The citizens fled to the island of Salamis, just off shore, and
the fleets gathered. Everyone, said Herodotus, prayed earnestly to

Boreas, the wind (remember the Kassite Burias). Themistocles, the
Athenian vice-admiral, surveyed the situation calmly. Realizing vic-
tory could be won only by superior cunning, he lured the tubby
Persian craft into narrow straits where they could not maneuver.
There the Greeks, master mariners to a man, cut them up at leisure.
And from his throne, set high on a hill so as to give him a clear view
of the expected Greek defeat, Xerxes beheld the ruin of all his plans.
Two later land battles completed the victory and sent the Persians
home for good and all.

Within fifty years of these two sets of victories, Athens—and in
reflected glory the rest of Greece—achieved the greatness that most
people remember when they speak of the glory that was Greece. In
that time flourished her greatest playwrights—Aeschylus, Sophocles,
Euripides; her greatest philosopher, Socrates; her greatest statesman,
Pericles.

In the lifetime of one man both beginning and end of the triumph
were played out. Socrates was born ten years after the victory at
Salamis. He came to manhood amidst the bustle and excitement of
those growing, glowing years. With his keen mind, his perpetual
seeking after wisdom, he became a sort of unofficial interrogator of
Athenian youth. Not really a teacher (he never gave answers), he
was nicknamed The Gadfly. And he was content with that. "What is
truth?" he asked of his listeners everywhere. "What is virtue?" And
the young men who prized his company strove to answer for him and
for themselves.

In 399 B.C., after Athens had first ruled, then ruined an alliance
of Greek cities; after Sparta had jumped at the provocation; after
the two cities had fought and Athens, at last, had been defeated and
her long walls torn down, Socrates and the golden years came to an
end together. He was murdered, judicially, by the Athenian courts

and the Athenian people, who, turned bitter and cruel in defeat, used him as a scapegoat for their troubles. All this he understood. Accused and convicted of impiety (and by a people never notably pious), he refused the opportunity to escape, thinking it better to die as he had lived, by his city's laws. Even so, he was the first man Athens ever punished so for his convictions and the last. His thoughts, which had so threatened and disturbed the people of a frightened Athens, lived on in the writings and teachings of his pupils Plato and Xenophon.

Sparta herself had not long to wave. To the astonishment of all Greece, she was defeated by an army of Thebans, never much in the military line. Thebes won by simply outflanking the phalanx, which no one had ever thought of doing before. And there was joy in Hellas, for Sparta had few friends.

And so the cities went on, a little narrower, a little poorer, living on glories past, contentious still. Athens was fast settling into the role she was to play throughout later times. She was becoming the schoolroom of the ancient world, while her short-lived time of glory became its model.

Somebody else had plans for the cities of Greece. And that somebody set about his task. Wily Philip of half-barbaric Macedon (the mountain land north of Greece) had a thirst for conquest. His son, Alexander, had that and something else besides. Alexander had for his tutor Aristotle, the scientist-philosopher. And he was in love with the epic poetry of Homer.

After 338 B.C. Philip and Alexander did bind the Greek cities at last (over Athenian protests). Most generous the Macedonians were, flattering, and with a nice respect for tradition. And then, with his army (which included a large Greek contingent) Alexander the King crossed the Hellespont. He intended to fight the Trojan War all over again, with Persia playing Troy and Darius III cast as Priam.

Very young, very beautiful, a superb tactician, and an irresistible leader, Alexander enjoyed the absolute loyalty of his men. With them he conquered everywhere—from Troy to Egypt, from Palestine to the Persian Gulf, from the sands of Arabia to farthest Bactria and beyond—down, down into mysterious India. He found himself in possession of an empire. Not just the old Persian Empire of Cyrus, but a good deal more besides. He was amazed and impressed by Persia's system of roads, her rapid communications, her imperial governing machinery, and the exotic look of her motley peoples.

Somewhere along the way, he had a new dream. It was a dream of one world, united under one law with each separate part nevertheless free to live and worship and govern itself very nearly as it chose. He dreamed of bringing the treasures of Greek civilization to these new people and of taking back to Greece their wisdom. And he wrote:

> I see in many nations things which we should not blush to imitate; and so great an empire cannot fitly be ruled without contributing some things to the vanquished and learning from them. . . .

Before his dream could be realized he died. He was only thirty-two, and he died of a simple fever aggravated by hardship, exposure, and overmuch wine. Already he was considered a god. His features—at least the features of Greek deities—adorned representations of the gods from Egypt to India.

His empire was divided among his generals, who achieved, each in his own domain, an approximation of that hybrid Hellenic culture Alexander had dreamed of. There was a great meeting of minds then, a pooling of gods, art, architecture, and beliefs, a widening of horizons. Ideas bounced about this new, larger world as merrily as sugar bubbles in a glass of champagne.

But peace and law were not yet won. Nations and kingdoms of this hybrid Hellas attacked one another with as much gusto as ever the old Greek cities had warred. It was not until later days that still another power brought to the ancient world the Roman Peace.

9. Rome

The Propagation

Whoever would have thought—looking at Rome in the year 490 B.C.—that it could ever be anything but what it was then, a rude little market town on the Tiber. While the Greek cities, with Athens in the lead, were fighting Persians, carving statues, writing plays, exploring ideas, and just generally glorying in those adventurous golden years, Romans stayed home and minded their farms. They traveled little, hated the sea, and seldom bothered with trade except in the simple farm goods they could bring to market.

The practical, hardheaded, rural turn of mind so characteristic of those early Romans is reflected in Latin words, many of which have acquired very different meanings with the passing years. *Cohort* (Latin, *cohors*) meant first a sheeppen, then the flock of sheep that

went in it, and last of all a flock of soldiers—a regiment. *Pontifex,* the Latin word for priest (from it comes *pontiff,* now a title of the pope), originally meant "bridge-builder." Presumably, the man who could properly span a stream possessed rather considerable spiritual powers. Even the word for "think"—*cogitare*—had a rural ring to it. It meant literally "to shake together" as one might shake peas in a sieve. Our word *pecuniary* recalls the inevitable Roman sheep. It still suggests finance—though our cash is in hand, not on the hoof. *Money* itself began with a flock of geese—the goddess Juno's geese, kept in her temple, which also housed the Roman treasury. Because of the loud cackling of her geese when a night raiding party of Celts attacked the city, the goddess was thereafter called the warner—Juno Moneta. Whence our *money.*

Roman names are either practical and unimaginative or frankly descriptive. Children were often simply numbered as they came along, especially after the fourth, when the ancestral given names ran out. Quintus, Sextus, Septimus, and Octavius were all favorites. Girls nearly always got the surname with a feminine ending: Livia of the Livius family, Julia of the Julians. Some famous family names came from not very flattering nicknames: Galba (fat paunch), Flaccus (flabby), Rufus (redheaded), Porcius (pig). Even the famous Cicero, still read by every struggling student of Latin, launched a distinguished career as an orator with a name that really meant "chick-pea."

The hick-town Romans were frankly deplored by their neighbors. The gay and elegant Etruscans from up north, for example, were particularly patronizing. They claimed a blue-blooded Anatolian ancestry dating back to Trojan War times, when (they said) they had come to Italy. (The Romans would later pre-empt this origin myth for themselves.) The Etruscans may have spoken sober truth. Although

Early Rome

they used Greek letters, the language of their writing has never been deciphered. It may yet prove to be one of the Anatolian tongues.

Actually, the Etruscans did not snub Rome entirely. They thought it expedient to install there a dynasty of Etruscan kings—the Tarquins—whom the native Romans eventually threw out and replaced with elected consuls and a republic.

To the south of Rome were the cities of Magna Graecia—many surpassing the Greek mother cities in size and splendor. Sybaris, for example, was to become forever a symbol of thoughtless, conscienceless, utter luxury. Syracuse, on the island of Sicily, faced the power of Phoenician Carthage just across the Mediterranean and defeated her on the very day—some say the very hour—the Athenians were vanquishing the Persian fleet at Salamis.

And then—almost before anyone could believe it had happened—the loutish little market town on the Tiber became the master of Italy and itself challenged Carthage in place of Syracuse.

It happened because—next to being farmers—the Romans were soldiers. Maybe they should better be called farmer-soldiers, or soldier-farmers. Certainly their ancestors had been warriors, charioteers, battle-ax wielders, long before they descended upon the Italian peninsula. And archaeological evidence from their central European starting point indicates they had taken to farming ways, too. Sometime around 1200 B.C. central-European Battle-ax folk began to expand violently in all directions. Perhaps it was the thrust of this original expansion that set other tribes in motion, sent them spilling into civilized lands and into the light of history, where they appear as the Phrygians, the Sea People, and the Dorians. It sent some groups percolating over the Alps. These were speakers of early Italian languages (of which Rome's Latin would be one).

By 1000 B.C. the Romans-to-be had settled into their land. They farmed it; they also fought over it and beyond it with undimmed enthusiasm. For they were warriors still. The first month of their year was named for the god of war because it brought warmer weather and the earliest opportunity for raids and battle (these began, of course, only after spring planting had been prudently done). That month is now our March.

Little by little, with unremitting practice in war, neighboring towns and neighboring peoples were annexed or bound to Rome with strong alliances. But there was something to this amalgamation besides military expertise. It was the whole of the Roman character that made the glue. The Romans were not brilliant, facile, and creative as were the Greeks. They did not value the play of minds. Their ideals were downright and plain: *religio,* binding oneself to something larger than one's self—in this case, the patriotic ideal of Rome; *humanitas,* respect for individual worth; *mores,* respect for tradition; *auctoritas,* respect for the law; *fides,* respect for honor; *disciplina,* the ability to govern oneself; and *severitas, gravitas, constantia*—all together conferring that grave and humorless demeanor, that stern dedication to duty which caused the gay Etruscans and the volatile Greeks to call the Romans dour.

But it was this dourness and this dedication to a standard of moral character (honored in the later days more in the breach than in the observance) which enabled the Romans to fight—and to lose—and still to win.

Pyrrhus, a king of Macedonia (long after Alexander), discovered this when he came to the aid of Greek cities besieged by Rome. Because of his experience, any military victory bought at a cost too high to pay is said to be pyrrhic. He won the battles; he couldn't win the war. Not only did the city of Rome survive defeat intact; Roman Italy came through, too. Netted now by a superb system of practical Roman roads, settled in stable alliances, and benefiting from a governing system which unified towns of Samnite or Etruscan or Latin origin and at the same time allowed them civic freedom, nobody wanted to defect. The whole peninsula felt itself to be one thing at last, an entity entire. Certainly this is more than Athens, with all her brilliance, all her dash, was ever able to bring off.

Hannibal of Carthage ran smack up against Roman character when he crossed the Alps and invaded Italy. He, too, defeated the Romans up and down the peninsula and stayed on the scene for a good number of years. And still he lost. Eventually Romans took to the hated ships, crossed the sea, and burned Carthage to the ground, thus destroying forever the threat from that quarter. Rome then inherited Spain and North Africa, and all the other Carthaginian possessions. As a result of the Macedonian Wars (three fought in roughly the same one-hundred-year period as the three desperate wars with Carthage—264–146 B.C.), Rome fell heir to Greece. Cisalpine Gaul had already been annexed. Then part of Asia Minor was willed by its ruler to the Roman Senate. The year was 133 B.C., and, all of a sudden, Rome found herself an empire.

The only trouble was that it was all too much of a good thing. And too soon. Roman people had always had the virtues of the poor and the proud. The Roman Republic had achieved a carefully adjusted system with enough built-in checks and balances to ensure representation of all classes and interests. In the beginning, of course, things had been different. Patricians had dominated the working people—the plebians, they were called. One day this group struck, decamped in a body, leaving all the menial work behind for the aristocratic leaders to do. Horrible thought! And so the plebians were lured back to work with the promise of being given their own spokesmen and protectors—tribunes who would have wide powers in the city government. Theirs was the ultimate power of the veto—"I forbid." At last the proud abbreviation SPQR really meant the Roman Senate *and* the Roman People. And everyone was pretty much satisfied.

Then, with the Empire, money started rolling in—more wealth than frugal, puritan Rome had ever seen, more than she knew what to do with. Gold and grain and the pernicious business of slaves—in the use of which Rome was no better than her neighbors and sometimes worse than most. Wealthy men got wealthier, and poor men poorer. Big landholders with many slaves quickly bought out or foreclosed small freeholdings. Wounded veterans arrived home to find their farms gone and their families in rags. The dispossessed and the unemployed flooded the city, where they were beguiled from their wretchedness by free grain and free gladiatorial games. Thought by Cicero and others to be "character building," these games grew ever more brutal as urban sensibilities became first blunted, then jaded, then numb. Beyond providing bread and games, nobody knew or seemed to care what happened to the army of unemployed. Two famous tribunes—brothers named Gracchus—worked to obtain reforms and were both killed for their pains. In these desperate times, even tribunes were no longer sacrosanct.

Practical Romans since the early days had hedged all battle bets by formally inviting the enemy's gods to switch allegiance to Rome, where they would be given bigger and better offerings. Now, in Empire times, the gods were flocking to Rome in wholesale lots and without official invitation. From Egypt came ever-popular Isis, Hellenized, no longer an elegant and elongated siren but a plump and modest matron holding a baby who sucked his thumb. From Anatolia came more mother goddesses: Cybele, whose rites shocked Roman sensibilities with their orgies of blood and mutilation, and ancient Ma. Later there was Mithras, favorite of the troops.

Nothing would do but that the world and all its ways be brought into the Roman Empire. And though the Senate hadn't quite got the knack yet of managing that empire effectively, the discipline and expertise of the Roman soldiers held what they took all the same. These soldiers were coming to be bound less to their lands (fast disappearing anyway) than to their generals, the imperators, who commanded them. They were less citizen-soldiers than battle-scarred professionals, out for pay and loot and a triumphant return home, led by their general in gorgeous parade armor and crowned with laurel.

An army of these professionals under Julius Caesar took all Gaul (now France) and Britain as well. After that they followed Caesar back to Rome, torn now with civil war, terrorized by proscriptions, hardly knowing which way to turn.

To earn the right to put things in order, Caesar had to fight off other armies of other Roman professional soldiers (under *their* generals). All around the Mediterranean Sea (Mare Nostrum—"our sea" —the Romans called it now) the power struggles progressed. When at last Caesar won out and came back to Rome, he barely had time to put the economy in shape, reorganize the machinery of government, and give employment to the poor before assassins' daggers put an end to his life (44 B.C.).

Julius Caesar had made a great mistake. He had put on airs. He had behaved like an emperor. And the Roman patricians, cherishing dreams of the good old days, could not bear it. They were perfectly willing, however, for Caesar's grandnephew and heir, Octavian (later Augustus), to wield an emperor's power so long as he did not behave like one. And he did not. He carefully deferred to the Senate in everything, complained of his burdensome duties, was entreated to remain, and did so through a long and devoted life. In his last years he was called the father of his country.

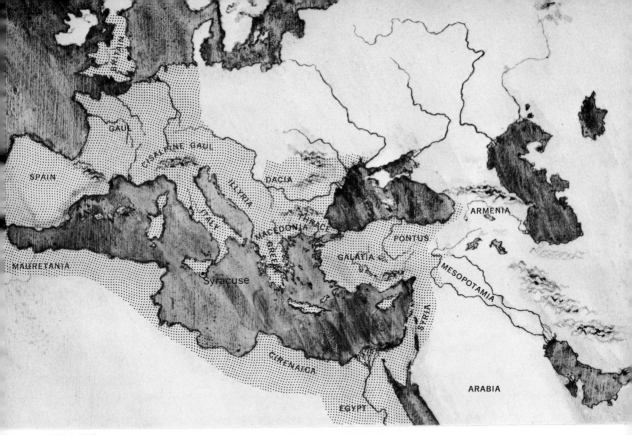

Roman Empire During the Reign of Trajan
(98–117 A.D.)

So well had he planned and organized for empire, so carefully had he installed a corps of civil servants in key positions, that his work survived a succession of crackpot emperors—those scandalous Caesars so well described by that master gossip of all time, Suetonius.

After the heirs of Julius and Augustus came the three sturdy, un-aristocratic Flavians. (Said the bluff, rueful Vespasian as he lay dying, "Alas, I think I am becoming a god." A last laugh at the custom of worshiping dead emperors as divinities. It was the patriotic thing to do.)

After Vespasian and his son came the philosopher-kings—Nerva, Trajan, Hadrian, Antonius Pius, and Marcus Aurelius (96–180 A.D.).

Altogether they gave the empire—which was then most of the civilized world—such a reign of peace and law that there prevailed at long last that fulfillment of which Alexander had dreamed: the world peace— now Pax Romana—with unity in diversity and protection under law.

The Pax Romana made possible the transmission of something more: the glory of Greek learning and Greek thought and Greek art. For here the Greeks had conquered their conquerors. Early in Republic times the influence of Greek writing and Greek architecture had begun to be felt; even the Greek pantheon was adopted wholesale. The new deities were helpful in personifying that vague Roman sense of the celestial in all things, and, of course, they were given Roman names: Zeus became Jupiter; Hera, Juno; Aphrodite, Venus; Poseidon, Neptune.

Later, Greek slaves were in heavy demand as private tutors, private doctors, private librarians. Every educated Roman had to be bilingual if he wished to retain his academic standing. Orators such as Cicero studied Demosthenes, and budding philosophers studied Plato. Old-timers, of course, ranted against all this newfangled Hellenizing, claiming it was weakening Rome's moral fiber, her ancient strain of puritanism. All things considered, it was probably the new wealth rather than the new learning which took its toll on Roman character. At any rate, things Greek went right on gaining vogue up to and during the time when barbarians sacked the city, nearly five hundred years later, and the empire shrank to its eastern half. There, in a Byzantine setting, visitors could observe the novelty of a Roman Senate conducting its business entirely in Greek.

People say imitation is the sincerest form of flattery, and it is primarily through Roman imitation that we have received our Greek heritage. Much of Greek art we know only through Roman copies. Greek literature was collected in the private libraries of Roman men of wealth and perpetuated by the Roman system of education. Even the works of Roman literary critics and commentators serve to put us in touch with the Golden Years.

If the artistic and intellectual brilliance of Rome was largely a reflection of Hellas, one thing was surely Rome's very own. Said the poet Vergil in his tale of the beginning of Rome:

> . . . Others will breathe life into bronze with more delicate art—I know it well—will carve marble into the visage of life, will plead cases better, will chart the orbits of the stars and foretell their risings. But your task, Roman, is this: to rule the peoples. This is your special genius: to enforce the habits of peace, to spare the conquered, to subdue the proud.

Rule Rome could, and rule she did, by her strength and steadiness, by her laws and her respect for law. These are her most direct legacy to us. Our whole judicial process is built on the Roman system. The right of jurists to interpret and define the law is Roman. So are the progression of litigation through courts of appeal; the concept of a citizen's inalienable rights; the passion for codifying and clarifying existing laws.

Our very words for legal concepts are Latin in origin. *Justice* comes from *ius*, which meant "law" or "right" in general. *Lex*, to which our *law* is related, referred to specific legislation. Our *jurisprudence*—"wisdom in the law"—is not far from the original in form or intent. And it is not just in derivative words that the Roman legal inheritance shows plain. The whole legal profession—today as always—swallows its Latin untranslated and underived. Its prodigal use of phrases such as *habeas corpus, res justae, pro forma,* and *a priori* tends to make legal documents all but unreadable to the awed layman with his non-classic education.

In government, the principle of checks and balances is Roman. And while—now as then—some slowing of state business results, it nonetheless provides the best protection yet devised for the individual citizen. Republican Rome set her two consuls—supreme executives elected for a limited term—to check each other while the Senate checked them both and the tribunes checked the Senate. Our system parcels out power among the three branches of government: executive, legislative, and judicial. But the same principle of checking and balancing is at work.

It was not only Roman law but Roman roads as well which knitted the far-flung empire into a piece. So well built were they, so lasting, that many are still in use though often too narrow for vehicles wider than sports cars. Because of those roads—with their way stations and government-run "motels"—tourism became a thriving business in empire times, and communications were as rapid as ever they would be until the invention of the steam engine.

Since the ultimate Roman triumph was in all things practical, one might expect much of Roman engineering. And one would not be far wrong. Their buildings, like their roads, were sturdy, solid, built to last. Though Rome borrowed most of her architectural forms from Greece, she turned to Asia for the dome and the arch, and made of both a triumph. The arch was used in monuments, buildings, and most strikingly of all, in aqueducts and bridges. Somehow the Romans

never got over their original reverence for bridge building. And to build still bigger, still better ones, they even invented a mortar which would harden under water.

Then there is the matter of language. When I opened my first Latin textbook, long ago, I found on the flyleaf a note written by a waggish predecessor. It said:

> Latin is a dead, dead language,
> It's dead as it can be.
> It killed the ancient Romans,
> And now it's killing me.

Perhaps my unknown friend would have suffered less (or considered that he suffered less) with French or Spanish. And yet, these and all the Romance tongues are forms in which Latin has been, not buried, but resurrected. Roman soldiers on garrison duty all over the far-flung empire often took native girls to wife and reared sons who, in their turn, enlisted in the Roman army. And it was the Latin they spoke with the broken accents of their mothers' tongues that has been preserved in the languages of France and Spain and Portugal and Rumania. Italian is Latin with a smack of the market place and the games and the common crowd.

Even English is not without its Latin patina. In the legal vocabulary it is pretty obvious, just as it is in medical and ecclesiastical terminology. But even in everyday speaking we can not go far without a Latin root or at least a sprinkling of prefixes.

Little did the young poet of the textbook know that when he *dated* his verse he was using Latin handily indeed. For our whole calendar is by courtesy of Rome and in itself tells a capsule story of the Roman way.

January, first month of our year, honors Janus, the double-headed god of doors. Of all the Roman pantheon, he was perhaps the most truly native—except for Saturn, who found his way into our week and marks each Saturday. February comes from Februo, the Roman month of purification, the time for burning rubbish both actual and magical, of casting out the bad and welcoming the new. March is for Mars, the Roman god of war. April comes from a word meaning "to open"— specifically, the opening of spring buds. And May comes from Maia, an ancient goddess of spring. June is for Juno, first the numen, the personification of each woman and all women, later queen of the Roman pantheon and patroness of marriage. June weddings are still popular in our day. July, of course, is in honor of Julius Caesar, and August commemorates his grandnephew. September, October, November, and December follow the Roman penchant for numbering when imagination failed to produce a name. They used to mark the months from seven to ten. And even though they now name the months from nine to twelve, they have kept their old numbers.

The legacy of Rome was not diminished even when the inevitable barbarians came from beyond the Rhine. For centuries the Roman economy had been·badly mismanaged. And after the philosopher-kings, corrupt leaders and public apathy had undermined the foundations of empire. With the invading hordes, the splendid shell decayed. Weeds grew in the Roman Forum. The city's population diminished. Throughout the empire, people began attaching themselves to whatever strong man seemed capable of offering the greatest protection. Most civilized settlements simply fell lock, stock, and citadel to the invading barbarians.

But knowledge of the old times did not disappear altogether. A dim remembrance of better days and better ways remained like a dream to give comfort to people once embraced by a mighty law. Citizens of much-shrunken towns retained the shadow of old guilds and associations and civic pride.

It was primarily in the Christian Church that Rome's fading genius was preserved. Long before the barbarians came, Roman law had been incorporated into canon law and Roman organization into ecclesiastical rule. Little by little the practical Roman way, coupled with the persuasive power of a new spiritual doctrine, reconquered for the Church all the land temporal Rome had lost. In monasteries and churches throughout Europe were hidden records of old times ready to hand when the darkness of the Middle Ages began to lift a little.

The Roman Catholic Church, too, failed to perpetuate the Roman Peace—as have all churches and all attempts so far. And yet the hope still lives in many hearts, now as then. It is a hope which binds us, the living and the dead, the past and the present. It is a hope which yet may bring again a Great Peace. Not the Pax Romana, to be sure, but still and all a peace for the civilized world—the whole of earth.

10.   Celts and Their Precursors

Settling Europe

Looming to the north, half enclosing the peninsular civilizations of Greece and Rome as they flowered, was the European hinterland, the Celtic world in which great Rome herself had deepest roots. In terms of history, it was a shadowy world, but it had never been without its tides of movement and events, and it was certainly not without people. The supreme artists of the old high hunting days, the days of the Old Stone Age, had lived and worshiped and painted in caves of France and Spain. Fisherfolk of the Middle Stone Age had congregated in settlements all along European coasts and rivers. And by 5000 B.C. the farmers had come, making their way along the Danube and into the heart of the continent.

A couple of millennia later the whole land mass was respectably

populated. In some places, indeed, farming villages were larger than such villages would be in medieval Europe, hundreds of years in the future. Primitive methods of clearing fields—the old system of slash and burn, plant, gather, and move on—had already altered the appearance of European forests. There had been time, after all, time for the land to change and for the groups of people who lived on it to develop each its own customs, each its own ideas about living.

In the eastern part of Europe, in what we now call the Balkans, farmers had found ways of keeping their fields fertile. Perhaps they rotated crops, letting some fields lie fallow; perhaps they used the manure from farm animals to fertilize the soil. Something of the sort must have been customary, because they and their descendants lived year after year, even century after century, on the same village mound, which grew ever higher as new houses were built on the ruins of old ones. Plainly these eastern-European farmers had ties to the land of their origin—ties to Anatolia. Their pottery styles, their seal stamps, and their fat and pleasant little mother goddesses were very like prototypes to the east and south. These were people without priests or kings, apparently, for neither temples nor palaces have been found among their remains. The goddess figures no doubt presided over hearth and home.

Farther west along the Danube were people of a different sort. Though they moved frequently to new land, the houses they put up were substantial ones, timber-framed and large—too large, too long to be single-family dwellings. Perhaps each was meant to shelter several related families, just as the long house of the Iroquois Indians of North America was meant to shelter a family "line"—grandmother, her daughters, their husbands and children. Whatever the social system of these European long-house people, they seem to have put all their energy into building and farming. No deity figures have been found in the ruins of their villages; grave goods were skimpy. Even their pottery was made strictly for use, not show.

If the people of central and eastern Europe were casual about their religious observances, the people of the west were not casual at all. By 3000 B.C. the coast line from Spain to Scandinavia and the interior along the Rhone River had been thoroughly traveled by ancient missionaries, spreading news of the Great Mother and hope of life everlasting. From settlement to settlement the missionaries went among all sorts of people, everywhere inspiring men to erect similar monuments and sacred places. Sometimes these were simply enormous single stones (megaliths) on which were scratched sacred symbols, or perhaps the outline of a giant female figure. More often they were great tombs in which all the dead of a community could be laid to rest, returned, as it were, to the Mother, there to await rebirth. For with the dead were deposited not just the usual pots and weapons and ornaments but emblems of the Mother, plaques bearing the holy signs. The community tombs took a variety of forms. Some were cut into rock cliffs; others were constructed of gigantic stone slabs or of smaller stones laid like brick in courses meeting in a vaulted roof above. Always the freestanding tombs were covered over with earth in mounds so high that some stood as tall as a five-story building. Many were equipped with forecourts which probably served as chapels. Altars have been found there, ceremonial stone bowls, and representations of the goddess. Sometimes these were merely pairs of enormous, stylized eyes. All-seeing eyes for the Mother of all? Perhaps.

The cult of the western megaliths apparently had its beginning in Spain not long before 3000 B.C. It may have come with colonists from the eastern Mediterranean, sent abroad perhaps to mine the metals in which the Iberian Peninsula abounded. No doubt the colonists met with a hostile reception, because they built fortress towns as well as community graves. Was home base in Anatolia? Was it Crete, where communal cave-tombs and round mortuary houses (tholoi) of brick and stone were common? Perhaps.

Into this Europe of tomb-builders, long-house farmers, and old mound villagers, there arrived, around 2000 B.C., two new groups of people—both of them restless and venturesome, neither of them much given to farming ways. From somewhere in Iberia came master copper-smiths (perhaps representing a fusion of Mediterranean colonists and native folk). The smiths were also archers and perhaps herders, but their real living was apparently earned in trade. They manufactured a curious sort of pottery beaker shaped something like a bell and because of it are known to us simply as the Bell Beaker Folk.

From the east came the Battle-ax People. Traveling in wagons and with their families, everywhere they left behind mementoes of their passage: the mounded single graves of their chieftains, their corded pottery, and where their paths lay across peat bogs and marshy terrain, actual roads made of logs.

Somewhere in middle Europe the two groups—Bell Beaker and Battle-ax—met and mingled and fanned out in new waves of migration. Most of all, they multiplied. The monopoly of Indo-European languages in Europe testifies to *that*. (Of course we do not know what language the Bell Beaker Folk used; it was somehow lost in the merger.) Many of the older farming folk were driven out or overrun. Some simply adjusted to the new way of life. But the megalith builders set out to convert the newcomers and seem to have had some small success. Bell Beaker Folk took to burying their dead in megalithic tombs, though with grave goods that were strictly Beaker in style. And on some of the tombs battle-axes and spirals were added to the usual designs.

The immediate result of the Battle-ax–Beaker mingling was a big upswing in metal use. Both the Alps and the Carpathians had rich ore deposits, and very shortly these were tapped by miners and master metal smiths anxious to please their chiefly patrons. Some of the

Battle-ax chieftains were soon doing better than others. Especially fortunate were those whose domains lay along the routes by which amber was brought out of the north to the rich cities of the Mediterranean. They profited by this trade and grew rich—rich in cows, in followers, and in the metalworkers they could command. They loved and required beautiful jewelry—pins, bracelets, armlets, ceremonial axes—quite as much as they required efficient battle weapons. Gold, shiny gold, they thought the most beautiful metal of all, and they had their smiths fashion drinking cups of it. Even their buttons were gold-covered. All these things were taken into mound-tombs, now rich two-roomed houses of stone cut to depict items that would normally appear in the house of the living chief: battle-axes, bows and arrows, and rich textile hangings.

Around 1300 B.C. groups of chieftains and metal smiths occupying central and eastern Europe began to expand into the lands around them. The old mound settlements went under after thousands of years of occupation. The expanding group had begun to make a new type of long bronze slashing sword which apparently they used to advantage. They had also begun to cremate their dead, depositing ashes in urns which were then buried in the time-honored Battle-ax way with wheels, wagons, horses, and all the rest. Because of their burial habits, they are called the Urnfield People.

Why they exploded into military action nobody knows. Perhaps they were after new metal sources. Perhaps they themselves were pushed by incoming nomads from the steppe. Whatever the reason, they soon spread over central Europe and some moved down into Italy—where their distant descendants would one day build Rome. This expansion of the Urnfield People may have been the trigger that set other hordes ravaging into Greece and the Middle East. The stirred-up traffic, however, was not all one way. Some of the invaders, grown homesick for old surroundings, returned from the Middle East to Europe, bringing along new craft ideas and perhaps the craftsmen themselves. With all the turmoil in the Middle East it is not surprising that artisans there would welcome employment by new patrons. Oh, the Europeans were barbarians, to be sure, but they were *rich* barbarians.

Spread of Urnfield Culture

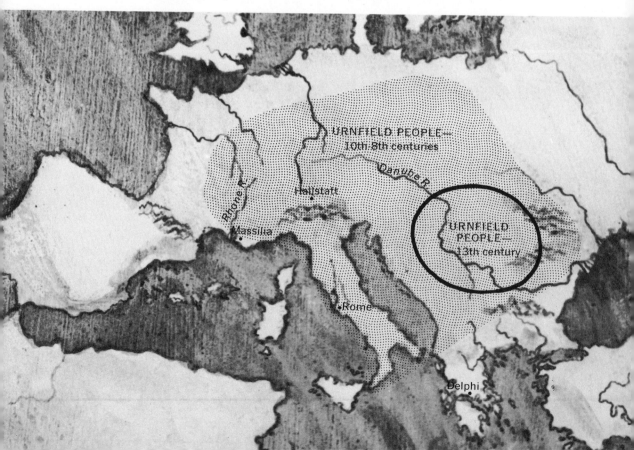

Some of the imported craftsmen must have been from Anatolia, because after 1200 B.C., after the Hittite monopoly had been broken, the knowledge of iron smelting came into Europe. Iron was used and used with great skill by successors, and perhaps descendants, of the Urnfield folk.

After 800 B.C., Europe begins to emerge tentatively from the obscurity of archaeology and into the light of history. At that time the new iron-using, iron-smelting folk of Europe were in contact with trading Greeks in Massilia (now Marseilles). Literate people in Greece soon began to hear vague rumors of these northern barbarians, knew at least that some wore pants like the Medes and rode in two-wheeled chariots. The barbarians of Europe also knew and were known to barbarians of the steppes. Some long-distance trading between the two areas seems to have been constantly in process, and some raiding too. Droughts in Scythian lands invariably sent Scythians ravaging into Europe.

What the iron-working barbarians called themselves we do not know. We can only name them archaeologically after the site where their most extensive remains have been uncovered. This site was near the city of Hallstatt in Austria, and so the ancient iron miners are called the Hallstatt People and their way of life the Hallstatt Culture. Cold, you will say. Nothing about *that* name to give us more than the barest outline of the real people, who lived and worked in Hallstatt twenty-six or twenty-seven centuries ago. But wait.

Wherever the miners dug for iron ore, there also did they dig for salt. Very often these iron-and-salt locations are uncovered in or near cities having ancient Indo-European names, names which include the word *hal* (as in Hallstatt). *Hals* is the old Greek word for salt. *Hal* is also "salt" in Celtic Welsh. It may be that folk more ancient than the Hallstatt miners scattered the place-of-salt names around central Europe. But if Hallstatt folk did indeed name the mines they worked (the names have survived into our own day) then perhaps they were Celts. Indeed, it is highly likely that they were, for their remains bear many resemblances to those of historical Celts who followed the Hallstatt folk in Europe around 500 B.C. The Hallstatt Culture also bears resemblances to that of the Urnfield folk, who lived earlier in central Europe (1300–800 B.C.). The Urnfield folk may also have spoken a Celtic language. Perhaps Celtic-speaking folk lived in Europe and Britain at an even earlier time.

Welsh—along with Breton and Gallic—is not the oldest surviving Celtic language. In terms of age, Old Irish (along with Old Scottish and Manx) occupies pride of place. Now the Old Irish word for salt is *sal,* and this is the original Indo-European root. Welsh, as we have said, uses *hal.* So different, in fact, are all the younger Celtic languages from Old Irish that many specialists believe there may have been as many as a thousand years separating the first Old Irish speakers in the British Isles from the first speakers of early Welsh. These seem to have arrived sometime around 500 B.C., but no one can be certain just when the Celtic ancestors of the Irish entered Britain. Perhaps even with the first waves of Battle-ax People.

This is the wildest kind of guess work, to be sure (though not entirely unheard of in linguistic circles). For the most part, sober students of archaeology and linguistics sternly resist the longing to put flesh and bone, historical connections, bright anecdotes, and a language where now only pots and relict words remain to mark the passage of human beings once brimming with tears and song. We must resist the temptation, too. Patience. Real people are on the way.

After 500 B.C. Celts can definitely be located in Europe and without a single doubt. Celtic chieftains were big consumers of Greek wine (enough Greek flagons have been found in Celtic sites to prove the point). Celtic craftsmen were busy at the forge, making beautiful animal figures in bronze and gold—figures astonishingly reminiscent in form and theme of Scythian art or that of the smiths of far-off Luristan. Once again Celts were on the move—bag and baggage, cattle and pigs, women, children, wagons, and all. Alexander of Macedon ran into some of them during one of his Thracian campaigns. Repeatedly Celts crossed the Alps to threaten Rome. In 279 B.C. they attacked Delphi in Greece and raged all the way down into Anatolia, where a whole province became known as Galatia because of them.

Apparently, *Celtae* and *Galli* (whence came the land-name, Gaul) were interchangeable terms for the whole people everywhere, though whether they called themselves by a common name or knew themselves as one entity nobody knows. The important sense of identity rested in the tribe, and there were lots of them, forever brawling with one another. A chieftain's wealth was reckoned first in cattle— never mind how scrawny the individual cow—next in precious metals and objects of art, and next in house size and accouterments. Honorable position was exactly reckoned in possessions. Greek and Roman writers found the Celts uncouth and barbarous, heavy drinkers, braggarts, touchy, prone to fight. Caesar, who fought the Celts first in Gaul (now modern France) and later in Britain, thought them incapable of forming rational judgments, too apt to follow hearsay or rumor, quick to take fright in battle, and undisciplined. Still, it must be remembered that Caesar was occupied with putting the Celts down and keeping up the will to war among the folks back home. Finding and naming the enemy's weak points were part of his job. Now and again, however, certain admiring contradictions creep through. Of Celtic politics he says:

A law, characteristic of the more efficient tribal constitutions, lays down that all foreign news of political importance, regardless of its source, must be reported to a magistrate, and must not be discussed with anyone else. For experience has shown that unfounded reports too often breed alarm. . . . All political discussion is banned except in a public assembly.

Certainly he gave grudging admiration to Celtic fort construction and siege tactics.

The Gauls are a most ingenious race, quick to borrow and develop any idea suggested to them by others. . . . They caught our siege hooks in nooses and hauled them inside [the fort] by means of windlasses. They also tried undermining the terrace, a job to which they brought all the skill acquired by long experience in the great iron mines of Gaul.

In Britain, where Caesar went in hot pursuit of highly placed Celtic refugees from Gaul, he found something else to admire. On the continent cavalrymen were riding their horses, but in Britain, the charioteer was still supreme.

Their skill, which is derived from ceaseless training and practice, may be judged by the fact that they can control their horses at full gallop on the steepest incline, check and turn them in a moment, run along the pole, stand on the yoke, and get back again into the chariot as quick as lightning.

From Greek and Roman sources we learn that the Celtic tribe, or *tuath,* was led by a chieftain-king (*rig,* like the Latin *rex* and the Sanskrit *rajan,* derived from the Indo-European *reg,* "the straight, true guide"). Tribesmen were divided into warrior nobility, ordinary folk, and serfs. There seem to have been few real slaves, though captured women certainly were treated as slaves. On a par with the knights was a professional class consisting of priests, artists and metal craftsmen, men of law, and poet-bards. These were honored as highly as the warriors and sometimes more so—artists for their skill, the others because they possessed the twin power of god and word. The priest could excommunicate, the bard could (and often did) ridicule. Vain kings, touchy of their reputations, took care that visiting bards were properly feted and entertained and rewarded. The contented bard might well work one's name and heroic deeds into the old epics he chose to sing. The offended bard could be counted on to compose a verse satire on the spot and then bruit it about later in other chiefly strongholds.

The unity of religion and of the priests, called Druids, was the only kind of over-all organization the Celts were ever to know. Every year they met in solemn convention at a spot reckoned to be the exact center of Gaul. Perhaps in time, had the Romans stayed away, some kind of secular, political organization, some drawing together of the tribes, might have emerged from this religious assembly. Who can say?

Caesar believed that druidical doctrine had originated in Britain, where Celtic students from Gaul were still sent for higher education. And since tribal kings held priests exempt from taxation or military service, there were always lots of candidates. Wrote Caesar of the druidical schools:

> . . . these young men have to memorize endless verses, and . . . some of them spend as long as twenty years at their books; for although the Druids employ Greek characters for most of their secular business, such as public and private accounts, they consider it irreverent to commit their lore to writing. . . . Their central dogma is the immortality and transmigration of the soul. . . . But they also hold frequent discussions on astronomy, natural philosophy, and theology . . .

And yet for all its poetry and art, its trained and cultivated priests, the Celtic religion was clearly barbarous in many ways. Human beings, reported Caesar, were sacrificed both in private rites and public ones. Criminals of one sort or another were preferred as victims, but lacking such, any innocent person would do. The Druids (claimed Caesar) foretold events by examining a fresh human liver rather than that of a sheep in the civilized Roman manner. And then there was the cult of the human head. Celtic tales that have come down to us are full of severed heads which, placed on stone pillars, sing, speak, and prophesy, and are, moreover, virtually indestructible. Stone representations of severed heads (with hand grasping the hair) have turned up all over France and Britain. Lintels, pillars, and memorial stones bear head decorations. Often the heads were represented with double or triple faces—an ancient motif which Celtic Italy must have retained until Roman times, when it appears as Janus, the double-headed god of doors.

Celtic chieftains were wont to collect the heads of their enemies and coat them in gold, an old steppe custom which Herodotus says was popular among the Scythians, who also liked to use enemy scalps for table napkins.

For their rites Celts preferred the open air or perhaps sacred groves to the confinement of stone temples. Bogs, ponds, even artificial shafts were also popular. In them art objects, precious metals, booty of all kinds, could be deposited in honor of the gods. Just what gods were worshiped we cannot know for sure. Because of the Roman (and Greek) habit of assimilating all deities to their own, the Celtic pantheon has prompted garbled descriptions. Caesar speaks, for instance, of a Celtic Mars, a Celtic Jupiter, a Celtic Diana, and so on. Celtic art, however, tells a somewhat different story. A stag-horned god, apparently named Cernunnos (the horned one), enjoyed a definite prominence. It may have been from this sad, forgotten old deity that Satan of Christian times acquired a set of horns.

There were Celtic goddesses, too. A favorite was Epona, goddess of horses, and a goddess-mare. (Mares, not stallions, were sacrificed by the Celts.) Though Celtic goddesses were seldom shown with their celestial spouses in the Roman manner, the female element was strong in Celtic myth, perhaps reflecting an ancient mingling of people and religious ideas in the days when the Mother of the Great Stones ruled in western Europe.

Much of what we know about Celtic myth and life comes to us from Ireland, which was never conquered by Rome—pagan or Christian. And when the new religion did gain a footing there, native priests and monks were sympathetic to the old lore and made sure it was preserved. It is through Irish and also Scottish lore that we have received our Celtic heritage. The old warriors of the British Isles with their boisterous natures, silver-tongued gift of gab, and strain of mystery live on in what we imagine the Irish national character still to be. (Whether it remains so because of the image or because it cannot be otherwise is anybody's guess.) Our use of words such as *blarney* and *leprechaun,* the playing of bagpipes at football games, the use of mistletoe (the Celtic plant of eternal life), a fondness for plaids—all these represent our Celtic heritage.

Soon after Caesar's time, the Celts of France, Spain, and England were Romanized. The battle-happy braggart, dirty-fingered and decked with gold, enemy heads bouncing on his chariot, was replaced, as Professor Stuart Piggott puts it, by the sober country gentleman who might speak his native tongue at home but who was thoroughly Roman in town. His country estate had central heating, and he wore a toga and collected art works from Italy. Celtic culture—whatever it might have been—died out quickly on the continent, but slowly, lingeringly in Britain. It was from the Celts, all tamed and civilized, that later invaders would learn, secondhand, of Rome, only in order to reject the tradition and begin again.

11. Teutons, Sarmatians, and Vikings

The Final Waves

German tribes beyond the Rhine exerted an irresistible appeal over the Romans of Caesar's time. Men of the legions might fear the Germans—certainly they had to fight those wild barbarians often enough. But all the same, they admired German courage in battle, German red hair, fierce blue eyes, height, and strength. It was, of course, recognized that the Germanic way of life was simple to the point of rudeness. What more could one expect of herdsmen who lived on the meat and curdled milk of their animals, who dressed scantily in skins winter and summer, who seemed to thrive on hardship? But, after all, they were brave warriors and sternly moral. The proper German was single-mindedly devoted to wife and children, openhanded in hospitality,

utterly guileless. Why, he even refused to drink wine, thinking it too soft, too refined. Simple? Yes, of course, but how refreshingly so.

For the cultivated Roman, baffled and enmeshed in the complex cares, the choices, the frightening nuances of civilization, German simplicity had a persuasive charm. It was a charm compounded by nostalgia. For this was the way Romans themselves had been in the days just before the early Republic and just after—stern, martial, virtuous—and they sighed for the good old days. Things were different now, of course. They had an empire whose frontiers were held by the superb discipline of a well-paid professional army. The ideal of the citizen-soldier and the simple life had long since flown.

The Romans liked the Germans as much as they disliked the Celts. The Celts, after all, had developed something approaching civilization—at least in terms of wealth and refinement of taste. They appreciated luxury and soft living, and in this they, too, reminded the Romans of themselves, of what they had become with wealth and security. It was a self-portrait they did not find particularly attractive.

Even in the little matter of horses the Germans could be depended on to behave in a characteristic manner, quite opposite from that of the Celts. Celtic love of fine horseflesh was proverbial. They took pains with breeding and imported beautiful mounts from abroad. Germans, on the other hand, did not care a hang what their horses looked like and, as a consequence, they were little and ugly, though strong. Service, not show, was the important thing. Even the saddle was rejected by German riders, who considered it effeminate.

A hundred years after Caesar's time, the Roman historian Tacitus was still saying much the same things about the German tribes. They had, in his day, taken up permanent abodes and a little farming, but this was left entirely to the women and old men. For, as Tacitus said, "They think it tame and stupid to acquire by the sweat of toil what they might win by their blood." Most of the time men lay about idly, awaiting the next summons to raid or plunder, the next hunt, the next gambling and drinking party (in a hundred years the Germans had at last taken to strong wine). Even so, Tacitus was still as impressed as Caesar had been with German strength of body and moral virtue and thought these tribesmen of all people in the world most uncorrupted by outside influences. They were, he said, without cities, without great wealth in metals and therefore scornful of wealth, suspicious of all but the oldest coins minted in Rome, those showing two-horse chariots on one side. German clothes were still of the simplest and scantiest sort. Among their weapons, only the precious shield—the shield that could be dropped only at the price of a man's life or honor—bore gay colors. Even funerals were simple. The chief, of course, was cremated with his horse and arms and the whole pyre buried in a great mound of earth. But there was very little weeping and wailing and hardly any display.

Caesar had pointedly noted the absence of priests and said that the Germans worshiped the sky, the sun, the moon, and fire in sacred groves or at lakesides, under the sky. By Tacitus's time priests had appeared and were busy doing everything from conducting services to interpreting omens conveyed in the snortings of a sacred white horse. As for gods, Tacitus contents himself with enumerating the usual Roman equivalents. (When the traditional religion found its way into writing, the chief gods were called Odin, Ziu, and Thor, or Donnar). For a certain Ertha, however, he attempts no equivalent. She seems to have been an old-style mother (perhaps it is from her name that we get our word *earth*). Ertha may possibly have been one of the ancient Vanir—traditional deities of field and farm whom the Germanic peoples added to their Aesir, or sky gods. Every year during a great peace, Ertha was pulled about in her cart to be feted and worshiped. (She may have been known as well to the Urnfield People, who made bronze images of such carts, the worshipers, and the goddess herself.) Tacitus says that the slaves who pulled the cart were later drowned in bogs. They were considered too contaminated by divinity to be allowed to live. Whatever informants Tacitus employed must have given him accurate information, for the bodies of just such victims as he described have been found today, completely preserved—hair, expressions, and all—in peat bogs of Germany and Denmark.

The Germans in Tacitus's time (about 100 A.D.) were what the Celts had once been. Like the Celts, they had no single name. The Germanni, from whom the "national" name derives, were probably more Celtic than German. Tacitus lists a great many German tribes who then inhabited Europe from Scandinavia to the Danube, from the Rhine to the steppes. He lists the Suevi (in Tacitus's day as in Caesar's the most numerous and powerful of all); the Chauci, who were strong enough not to have to fight; the Suiones (Swedes?), who sailed the ocean in oar-driven ships; the Teutones (from whom the language name derives); the Sitones (who were, to the utter disgust of Tacitus, ruled by a woman); and many, many more. Some, such as the Vandilii (Vandals), the Langobardi (Lombards), and the Gothones (Goths—ruled, said Tacitus, by kings and more strictly than the other German tribes), were to be tied to the later destiny of Rome.

As early as Augustus's time the Romans had decided to leave the Germans unconquered, to halt at the Rhine. One tribe or another was forever trying to cross into Gaul, but the frontier held firm, perhaps as much the result of happy circumstance as of military effort—a fact recognized by Tacitus, who added:

May the tribes, I pray, ever retain if not love for us at least hatred for each other; for while the destinies of empire hurry us on, fortune can give no greater boon than discord among our foes.

But the first threat to the Roman Empire came not from the Germanic tribes along the Rhine but from the east—from the Sarmatians of the steppes, who lived, as Tacitus wrote, "in wagons and on horseback." They were much like the Scythians in language and customs (except for the fact that Sarmatian maidens fought alongside their men, an unheard-of thing among the Scythians) and everywhere after 335 B.C. replaced them. They assumed what had been Scythian lordship over the agricultural Slavs and over the last Celtic

remnant in the east. They exacted tribute from the Greek cities along
the Black Sea and patronized Greek jewelers and goldsmiths as the
Scythians had been wont to do. Like the Scythians, they were ad-
dicted to the old animal art—stags, horses, and fantastic amalgams—
but they liked jewelry to be colorful, set with lots of pretty bright
stones. Greek artisans adjusted to meet the demand.

Sometime around 174 B.C. the Massagetae, Indo-European nomads
who had formerly lorded it over the Central Asian steppes and harried the Persian frontiers (it was they who had killed Cyrus), were
resoundingly defeated by the Huns, Turco-Tarter nomads from the
eastern steppes. The broken remnants of the Massagetae hordes fled
to their cousins, the Sarmatians, who absorbed the refugees, learned
from them, and enhanced the growing Sarmatian might. Tales of their
power and invincibility spread abroad even to China, which sent a
diplomatic delegation across the steppe to beg for Sarmatian aid in
controlling the ravaging Huns. From the Massagetae, the Sarmatians
picked up the habit of wearing body armor—fishlike scales of metal
sewn on leather. From the Huns they borrowed a new weapon—a
bone-reinforced bow and a heavy arrow with a three-edged head.
Newly equipped and enlarged, they moved west. By 20 A.D. they were
pounding at the Danube frontiers of the Roman Empire. With the
inconstancy of nomads they changed alliances on the slightest whim.
Sometimes, joining Roman armies, they flew in hot pursuit of the
rebellious Dacians, who lived in what is now Rumania. More often,
however, they and the Romans were on opposite sides. For years and
years—the Sarmatians fighting alone or with the help of the eastern
German tribes—the struggle continued. So fierce were they as op-
ponents, so implacable, that six Roman emperors were proud to add
the title "Sarmaticus" to their names. There is no telling how many
tribute troops were exacted from temporarily beaten Sarmatians to

bolster the armies of Rome. During the campaigns of Marcus Aurelius (175 A.D.) fifty-five hundred Sarmatian horsemen were sent to Britain, there to live out their lives fighting the barbarians from the north.

It was not the Romans who scattered the Sarmatians, however. The Goths were to blame. Already in Tacitus's time (whether he knew it or not) these German-speaking people from near the Baltic were on their way south. And no wonder. Tales of winter warmth and sun must have rung with irresistible appeal in frostbitten Gothic ears. Nobody can be forever in love with hardship, whatever Caesar and Tacitus may fondly have believed. By 250 A.D. the Goths (divided into eastern and western groups—Ostrogoths and Visigoths) were in Dacia overwhelming both Sarmatians and Romans and setting up a kingdom of their own. Soon they, too, were patronizing the Black Sea artists, requiring them to make yet another switch in technique (from jewel to enamel inlay) and in theme (from stags to birds of prey). The Romans simply enrolled the Goths as confederates in the Empire and gave *them* the task of guarding the frontier—there was not much else they could do at that point but make the best of things.

Meanwhile, back on the Rhine, some of the German tribes were massing, concerting as Tacitus feared they might. The members of the new amalgams called themselves Franks, or "freemen"; Allemani, or "all-men." Still the Gallic frontier held.

Their cousins, the Goths, were not to remain long in the warm lands around the Black Sea. New pressures were building up in the steppes beyond. The terrible Huns, who (as one writer put it) ate, drank, and held council on horseback, were on their slow way west. In 360 A.D. they crossed the Don and in 375 broke the Ostrogoths, subjected the Germanic tribes to their will, or sent them flying west.

For long years Indo-European nomads had roamed at will over the plains of Central Asia—some as far as the frontiers of China. But now they were all being swept out by the Huns, people at least partly Mongoloid in features and Turco-Tartar in language.

Edward Gibbon, the most famous chronicler of Rome's decline and fall, equated both the Hunnic hordes and the later Mongol hordes of Genghis Khan with the Scythians, and though his linguistic and chronological information was in error (by the time of the Hunnic invasion the Scythians had long since vanished from the scene), he was right in one important respect. The cultures of Scythians, Huns, and even Mongols were very much the same—the same in terms of food, clothing, and shelter; the same in terms of warfare, weapons, and battle trophies. The worship of sky and sun, thunder and rain was the same. So were the chiefly burials. In the Altai Mountains of Central Asia, a number of such burials have been found, dating to 450 B.C. Around these burials were the remains of tall Persian horses, grain-fed and hand-raised for sacrifice. In one tomb were two bodies completely preserved in ground ice: a tall lady of European features and a sturdy Mongoloid chieftain, killed in battle, scalped by his enemies, but buried with an artificial scalp tenderly sewn to his pate by devoted followers. Buried with them were splendid works of animal art, some on rich fabrics, some tattooed on the skin of the chieftain himself in faithful continuation of the old Scythian custom.

Perhaps Attila, the vivid leader of the Huns of 430 A.D., looked something like the chieftain of the Altai grave. A Gothic historian of the time says he was swarthy and had a large head, a flat nose, small eyes, and a scanty beard. (The Altai chieftain had been given a false beard of dyed horsehair.) He was also broad-shouldered, short-legged, and a superb horseman. A brilliant man, he was prone to be indulgent with enemies and wily in negotiations. His armies conquered all the way to Gaul and then he marched on Rome, because, it is said, of a lady's request—a Roman lady carted off to Byzantium and chafing in confinement.

Actually, the Visigoths, pushed before the Huns, preceded Attila to Rome. In 410 A.D. they treated the great city to its first sacking. The Germanic Vandals—who had swung through Gaul and Spain (where the province of Andalusia bears their name) and into North Africa—recrossed the Mediterranean in 455 to give Rome an even more ferocious taste of murder and rapine. (To this day the word *vandal* denotes a person who wantonly wrecks and destroys simply for love of destruction.)

The Huns, who had the worst reputation of all the barbarians, never got to Rome at all. Just outside the city they were confronted by Pope Leo I, an imposing figure of a man. What he said to the pagan Attila was not recorded, but it must have been effective, because Attila withdrew into Hungary where, after another year, he died (453 A.D.).

Like a great tide, broken into eddies and sucking backward into the sea, his army retreated along the way it had come. Some Hunnic groups tarried in the Balkans and in Russia, where they were augmented from time to time by fresh groups of Turco-Tartars. In Hungary, the very vortex of the Hunnic tide, a non-Indo-European language is still spoken. And to this day the flat, wide cheekbones, the straight black hair, and the eye folds of the invader can be seen on Slavic faces. "Scratch a Russian and you find a Tartar," the old saying goes, and there is a lot of truth in it.

The Germanic tribes shook free of the Hunnic yoke imposed on them in 375 and renewed the attack on crumbling Rome. It had taken them nearly four hundred years of constant assault to bring down this greatest empire of the ancient world. During the early days of empire, Roman troops had held like a rock against the breaking waves of barbarians. And not only against barbarians but against the incursions of familiar Persian enemies in the Middle East. In time, however, there were simply not legions enough. Trajan began to incorporate barbarian soldiers into his armies. Some were demanded as tribute troops and transported to bases far away from their native homes. Sometimes whole tribes were allowed to cross Roman frontiers and settle with the clear understanding that they would guard those frontiers from further incursions. In the time of Marcus Aurelius a plague came from the east to decimate the already dwindling armies. Marcus, that gentle philosopher, scandalized haughty Rome by enlisting criminals and slaves as troops. He was eager to add their Romanness as well as their numbers to an army fast becoming anything but Roman in ethnic composition. Things grew worse. Rome consumed more than she produced; she was both supported and protected by the provinces. Provincial citizens resented the grinding taxation, and provincial soldiers soon came to be a law unto themselves. When weak emperors wore the purple, the legions snatched at power, crowned their own generals, demanded bribes, became less disciplined and less skillful.

More and more barbarians came. Walls were raised to keep them out. Walls that stretched from the Rhine to the Danube; across the neck of Scotland; across the Balkans. Far at the other end of the steppes, the Chinese also built walls against their own barbarian tides and with just as little success.

To stem the tide, emperors used their treasure, buying time, buying safety. They tried intrigue, turning one ravaging tribe against another. They tried first to Romanize then to Christianize the invaders, hoping that would have a softening effect, and in some cases it did. Proudly and humbly, too, Odoacer, whose father had been Attila's councilor, and Theodoric, King of the Ostrogoths, thought themselves the saviors and preservers of Rome, fought and won her battles, and were assassinated for their pains.

Often the Romans tried marriages of state, promising their sisters and daughters to barbarian chieftains, and took German girls as concubines if not as wives (Roman law specifically forbade that). The Chinese, too, had tried the marriage remedy. One sad little poem, written in 110 B.C. by Princess Hsi-Chun, tells it all.

> My people have married me
> In a far corner of earth:
> Sent me away to a strange land,
>   To the King of the Wu-Sun. (Scyth? Hun?)
> A tent is my house,
> Of felt are my walls;
> Raw flesh my food,
> With mare's milk to drink.
> Always thinking of my own country,
> My heart sad within.
> Would I were a yellow stork
> And could fly to my own home.

Wherever the invaders landed they settled down to stay and enjoy, putting on superficially civilized airs to impress their new subjects, remaining bluff old warriors among their own fellows. They picked and chose among the new luxuries while living as much as possible in the old manner. More often than not they refused to take up residence in towns but built fortified settlements just outside. Christianity, when they accepted it, was often just a veneer to cover older ideas and customs. Kings and chieftains as late as 481 were gilding enemy skulls and being buried with battle-axes and treasure and the heads and hides of favorite mounts.

By 500 A.D. the Western Roman Empire had been wrecked for good and all. On its Italian ruins sat the Ostrogoths (soon to be supplanted by the savage Langobardi). Spain was Visigothic, Gaul belonged to the Franks, and in England were the Anglo-Saxons, Teutonic tribes from the northern coasts of Europe who, after years of ceaseless raiding, had at last found a home. The combined Huns and Slavs—now called Bulgars—threatened the Eastern, or Byzantine, half of what had once been the mightiest empire on earth. For all the efforts of the Christian Church, Europe in the Dark Ages was more Battle-ax barbarian than civilized Roman and, to a greater or lesser degree, it was to remain so through medieval times, until the Renaissance brought back classical learning.

Everywhere society settled into lines long familiar in forest and steppe. The king passed around the fruits of conquest to his followers and they to theirs. The man of means never forgot he was a warrior first and a landed gentleman only second, and that his lands and people existed merely to support his military contribution. People belonged to the priesthood, the knighthood, or were serfs, fit only to produce food for others. Traders and businessmen, the whole varied middle class of Rome, had vanished as utterly as the old aristocracy. What artisans there were, took refuge in some king's court or in holy orders. The education of a young man of good birth was still of much the same sort that Tacitus had observed among the German tribes four hundred years before:

> . . . . lads attach themselves to men of mature strength and of long approved valor. It is no shame to be seen among a chief's followers. Even in his escort there are gradations of rank, dependent on the choice of the man to whom they are attached. These followers vie keenly with each other as to who shall rank first with his chief, the chiefs as to who shall have the most numerous and the bravest followers. It is an honor as well as a source of strength to be thus always

surrounded by a large body of picked youths; it is an ornament in peace and a defense in war . . . . When they go into battle it is a disgrace for the chief to be surpassed in valor, a disgrace for his followers not to equal the valor of the chief. . . . The chief fights for victory; his vassals fight for the chief.

During the Dark Ages and medieval times judicial perplexities were often decided by omens, by ordeals, or by single combat in the old German manner. Sometimes quarrels about boundary rights or treatment of another man's serfs erupted into blood feuds which the king was usually unwilling or unable to do very much about.

The bearing and equipage of the mounted knight were simply an elaboration of the old Sarmatian pattern. It is, after all, but a short step from the Sarmatian warriors who, said Tacitus,

> . . . . wear coats of mail formed with plates of iron in the tough hides of animals, impenetrable to the enemy but to themselves an encumbrance so unwieldy that he who falls in battle is never able to rise again . . .

to medieval knights, who had to be cranked by pulley into their saddles.

Art belonged to the Church and to the monastery school and to heraldry. And there—on coats of arms—the old animal art of the steppe flourished once again in fantastic griffins, lions rampant, stags with branching horns. And when sculpture and architecture once again appeared, the old figures became gargoyles on the soaring eaves of the cathedrals we call Gothic.

The last of the Battle-ax People to terrify and harry Europe were the Vikings—another general name for the Teutonic-speaking tribes of Scandinavia. Nobody knows what the name really means. The Vikings substituted boats for chariots in chiefly graves and exhibited a somewhat greater interest in plunder than in war. Otherwise they conformed to the old catalogue of culture traits. What is more, they really got around. From the Baltic they made their way down the great rivers into Russia, where they dominated the local folk and laid the foundations for future ruling dynasties. They sailed across the Black Sea to Constantinople, where they alternately threatened and served Byzantine emperors as their Varangian Guard. Vikings even traveled by land and river to the Caspian Sea and down into Mesopotamia. Everywhere they were traders as well as raiders, and they were willing to trade anything—even human cargo. So often was this particular cargo Slavic that the name got into Western vocabularies as "slave."

On Atlantic shores, Vikings were equally aggressive. Early in the ninth century they took for themselves a large part of what had been Gaul, then Frank-land, then France. Their part became the Duchy of the Northmen, or Normandy. They sailed south and took a share of Sicily. A Viking king ruled for a time in Northern Ireland and another —the great Canute—in Saxon England. Sometime after 981 (when Erik the Red discovered Greenland) Viking ships touched base in the New World and left a colony or two to be lost or, in time, absorbed into the Indian world.

Huns had once been called the scourge of God. There are some who would say Vikings were more deserving of the title. And yet, for all their destructiveness and cruelty, Vikings have left to the West an undying heritage.

Vikings at home held local meetings called "things" and great tribal assemblies called "allthings" at which political and legal matters were discussed and various leaders elected. (Ziu, who seems to have been much like Mitra, the god of contracts, was the patron of "things.") The king usually acted as moderator at these meetings, for there he was merely first among equals and no autocrat by any means. The Vikings who colonized Iceland in 870, however, had no king and never acquired one. An elected "law-speaker" presided over the assembly, and priests kept track of the proceedings. Survivals of this old custom on the Isle of Man show us that the "thing" was rather like the town meeting in rural America. The Icelandic colony was very much a republic—and the first in the new barbarian Europe.

And yet the existence of assemblies among the Vikings is perhaps simply a reflection of something which, among most of the Battle-ax folk, was a tradition as strong as that of powerful and autocratic chieftains. Tacitus found this tradition at work among the Germans.

> The chief . . . is heard merely because he has influence to persuade. If his sentiments displease them, they reject them with murmurs; if they are satisfied, they brandish their spears. . . . In their councils an accusation may be preferred or a capital crime prosecuted. . . . In these same councils they also elect the chief magistrates, who administer law. . . .

The Anglo-Saxon Witanegemot (the king's council)—perhaps even the old Hittite pankus—may be in the same tradition. Though barbarians admired and followed the strong man and would do so more and more until among some peoples his power was absolute, still there existed as an alternative the form for public meeting and for talking things out.

It may be in just such a traditional barbarian assembly that Greek democracy had its roots. It may be from just such a background that The Roman Republic took shape. Though the final waves of European intruders brought to ruins what their own distant relatives had built, the pattern remained. In it lay the promise of a world wherein men would one day rule themselves, and of a civilization reborn.

Epilogue

A Capsule History of the English Language

> Sumer is icumen in:
> Lhude sing cuccu!
> Groweth sed and bloweth med
> And springth the wude nu.
> > Sing cuccu!

That's English. And English of not so terribly long ago, when you consider the wide view we have been taking of time in these chapters. That little poem was written around 1225 A.D., and, with some slight effort, its meaning can still be read. Roughly, it is: Summer is coming in: Loudly sings the cuckoo! The sod grows, and the meadow blossoms and the woods revive now. Sing, cuckoo!

Shakespeare's English is fairly close to our own. His words and his plays are still read, still performed, still popular. We can easily understand

> > > We are such stuff
> > As dreams are made on; and our little life
> > Is rounded with a sleep.

Or even

That time of year thou mayst in me behold
When yellow leaves, or none, or few, do hang
Upon those boughs which shake against the cold,
Bare ruin'd choirs, where late the sweet birds sang.

It was into the English of Shakespeare's time that the Bible was rendered in the version authorized by King James. And no English translation before or since can match it for beauty and power. Remember

The Lord is my shepherd; I shall not want.
He maketh me to lie down in green pastures:
He leadeth me beside the still waters,
He restoreth my soul.

But when we go back, back to the Anglo-Saxon beginnings of English, we find a foreign tongue. We need a translator. Consider this line from the *Saga of Beowulf,* a sort of early version of Jack, the Giant-Killer:

Gewat tha ofer waeg-holm, winde gefysed,
Flota fami-heals, fugla gelicost.

It says, "Then went over the billowy ocean, driven by the wind, the floater (ship) with foamy neck (prow), very like a wild fowl." Between then and now—what happened?

First of all, English did not have the same kind of straight-line development as did Greek, the most ancient words of which are still comprehensible to the modern Greek reader. It was in a succession of levels that English grew—rather like a seven- or even nine-layer-cake, with lots of rich filling in between. And the first three layers were baked before ever the Anglo-Saxons appeared in middle Europe, much less on the shores of Britain.

The pan for our language batter was England, that little island, that "precious stone set in the silver sea" (as Shakespeare called it). Separated as it was from the mainland, one would expect it to have languished in isolation. But no. It might just as well have been Grand Central Station for all the word traffic it sustained.

For time out of mind, the original hunting people had lived there, mining high-quality flint from the chalk cliffs and manufacturing from it a really superior line of tools. These first inhabitants were joined (as we have already seen) by a complement of Neolithic farmers. Some were part of that wave which fanned out from the Danube basin. Some, perhaps, arrived from down the coast by long sea voyage, surely a part of the missionary group that brought to western Europe stone-built community graves and the worship of a mother goddess. In England circles of upright wooden posts (some dating to 2500 B.C.) and circles of stone perhaps functioning as "temples" seem to be connected in some way with the tomb rites. The outer circle of old Stonehenge (only the holes remain) was very likely a result of missionary inspiration.

Still later the Bell Beaker Folk made their appearance, fanning out through the island, to be joined by successive warrior waves of mixed ancestry. You will recall that Beaker Folk and Battle-ax People met in central Europe about 2000 B.C. and mingled both bloodlines and ways of life. Moving west again, this motley crew reached the sea and crossed it to settle and thrive in England. There some of the old farming folk were dispossessed, and the community grave making diminished. Something about the old religion must have proved congenial to the intruders, however, for the rich warrior chieftains added to the old sacred places. It was they and their successors who had massive stones brought from afar and set on end to form great circles and horseshoes in the midst of the ancient monuments. The evidence of building and rebuilding, extending and refurbishing is still to be seen at Stonehenge.

Stonehenge is thought by some scholars to have been a kind of giant calendar, a fixed observatory by which the exact position of the sun at its solstices could be accurately plotted, or perhaps eclipses foretold. This fits in with what we know of the Battle-ax People and their veneration of the sky and sun.

The beginning of this renovation of Stonehenge dates to about 1500 B.C. Rich chieftains of that time were already in contact with the civilized world. Blue glass beads from Egypt, gold cups from Mycenae, and other exotic Mediterranean items were presented to the warrior chieftains of southern England. And there is something more to underline the connection. On one of the giant uprights at Stonehenge there was cut the outline of a dagger, Mycenaean in style. Could engineers from the Aegean have helped with the building of the monument? In any case, the presence of Aegean folk in Britain is not very surprising. This was, after all, the time of the high Bronze Age, and the rich tin mines of Britain drew seafaring traders as a magnet draws iron.

The merged languages of the hunters and the farmers and the Beaker and Battle-ax folk (with perhaps some trading terms thrown in for good measure) formed the first layer of our English cake. From it a few words have struggled upward to our present-day level. *Crag, down* (meaning meadow), and *ton* are some, together with a few place names.

The next language layer came with the Celts. Though we know very little about the earlier languages of the islands, we know a good deal about Celtic because it is still spoken in the British Isles, and (as we saw in Chapter 10) spoken in two varieties, one seemingly of greater age than the other. This tells us that the Celts came in waves and not all at once. It may be that the older languages of Britain (those of the Battle-ax People, at least) were related to those spoken by the incoming Celts, because Celtic very quickly established itself everywhere as the "native" tongue. It was not even dislodged by Latin after the arrival of first Julius Caesar's, then Claudius's legions.

Britain soon became as settled and prosperous a Roman province as Gaul. Roman roads ran everywhere (some are still in use). Roman walls kept out the Painted People, the wild Pictish barbarians from the north. Roman baths and Roman villas were built. But, unlike Gaul, Britain did not preserve its Roman words after the Romans left. A few remain from that layer, however. *Castrum,* the Roman word for fortified camp, became the later *castle.* The words *street, cheese, pepper, butter, inch,* and *pound* come from the Latin of that time. The Roman Londinium became London. Roman Eboracum became York, though possibly the town and its name date even further back, to pre-Celtic days.

It was around 400 A.D. that the Roman legions were withdrawn from Britain to defend the imperial city from the invading Teutonic tribes. Britain was having Teutonic troubles of her own. Anglo-Saxons from what is now Denmark and part of Germany had long harried the coasts of eastern Britain, always arriving when spring brought good sailing weather. With the legions gone, they grew bold enough to make permanent settlements along the coast, from which they could raid the rich towns of the interior at leisure. Helpless and bereft, the Romanized Celts mobilized around one Arthur, a local strong man (and hero of a hundred later legends). He defeated the Anglo-Saxons so soundly that full-scale invasion was postponed for fifty years.

But in time they came, the new invaders, and came to stay. They were divided into three tribes: the Angles (from whose name came England—"Angle-land"), the Saxons, and the Jutes. Many Celts fled to Wales, to Cornwall, to Brittany across the Channel, to relatives in Ireland or Scotland. Those who remained were bent to Teutonic words and Teutonic ways. And with this we are back to *Beowulf.*

English did not stay Anglo-Saxon entirely, because the cake was not yet half finished. New words followed new invaders. They were Vikings, this time, Danes—cousins to the Anglo-Saxons who had preceded them. Hardly had the Angles and the Saxons settled in when the Viking raids commenced. For a short time a Viking king even sat on the English throne. Good King Alfred and later Harold (last of the Saxon kings) drove the Danes out for good but not before they had left a layer of words behind. *Hit, loose, skin, knife,* and *husband* are some. They are words, like those of the Anglo-Saxon layer, meant to express homely, everyday things.

Finally came the Normans, who conquered so thoroughly that no invader ever landed again on English shores. The Normans (as we have seen) had been Vikings themselves originally ("Norman" is really a contraction of "Northman"), and they had cut out for themselves a large portion of northern France. In the course of time they became as French as the king in Paris, and French was the language they brought with them into England. By that time people were beginning to be conscious of legal niceties, so the Norman Duke William worked up what he considered a valid claim to the English throne, and over the Channel he went.

After the victory, Anglo-Saxons were badly treated. Many were reduced to poverty and servitude, and ill feeling was profound. The new gentry went about speaking Norman French, but the sturdy peasantry clung stubbornly to what had now become the "native" Saxon tongue. In time the Norman overlords had to learn it, too.

By the time they did, however, *Saxon* was *English* and much more congenial to the Norman tongue and the Norman mind. Quantities of anglicized Norman words had been added, so that one had a choice of two synonyms for nearly every idea. And one still does. Invariably, the simple term is of Anglo-Saxon origin, while the fancy one is Norman.

In the matter of housing, for example, *hut* and *cottage* refer to the same size dwelling, approximately. But the Norman *cottage* is by far the more elegant in connotation. Fancy people don't stay in summer huts, whatever the appearance. They stay in cottages.

Help and *aid* make another pair. *Aid* is the kind of assistance which applies between gentlefolk who really are not all that desperate in the long run. In the face of real danger, however, nobody cries, "Aid! Aid!" Oh, no. "Help! Help!" is the indispensable, the Saxon expression.

The whole situation can be neatly demonstrated in the food department. The Saxons had to care for animals on the hoof and in the stable; the Normans got the meat served to them on the table. So the

SAXON	Ox	Calf	Swine	Sheep	Deer
NORMAN	Beef	Veal	Pork	Mutton	Venison

language in which one kills an animal is not the same language in which one eats it. The same social distinctions apply in the matter of meals. By a scrutiny of word origins, one can see who ate what and when.

SAXON	Breakfast
NORMAN	Dinner, Supper, Feast

With the Renaissance a new layer of words came to English. It was a peaceful penetration this time. The power behind them was simply the potency of new ideas. Because Italy had given birth to the Renaissance, a good many Italian expressions, words describing the new arts and graces and learning, crossed the Channel and were Anglicized.

Sonnet and *balcony* and the elegant fluttery phrase "Dear me!" (from *Dio mio!*) are some. Names of musical instruments such as *viola* and *piccolo,* and musical terms such as *opera* and *cantata* came too. Even a few military terms arrived, and from them we have *regiment, brigade, colonel, infantry,* and *cavalry.*

With the rediscovery of the ancient classics, both Greek and Latin flowed anew into the language. Greek gave names to nearly all the new scientific ideas coming into being. Many stars and constellations came to be known by Greek names, and most of the new medical and surgical ideas were expressed in Greek. This process has not only continued into our own time; it has accelerated. When paleontologists unearth new fossils, when physicists formulate new laws or concepts, when biologists discover the secrets of life, the names for these are often drawn from Greek sources. Hence we have *Cynognathus, Aegyptopithecus; atom, electron, cybernetics; chromosome, antibiotic.* Greek, too, are the names given to the specialties in science (anthropology, psychiatry, pediatrics). About half our modern scientific and medical vocabulary is Greek in origin, sometimes appearing as hybrid terms which include Arabic or Latin roots.

The language of pharmacy derives from Latin almost entirely. Perhaps the practice of giving Latin names to drugs and medicines dates from the Middle Ages, perhaps from even earlier times. Latin, after all, was the exclusive language of learning for a very long time, even after it ceased to be a spoken language. And Latin words had been finding their way into English long before the Renaissance. Churchly words such as *consecrate* and *archbishop* derive from Latin terms that came in with the conversion of the Saxons to Christianity. Others—particularly those having to do with legal matters (*justice, jury, judge, court*)—derive from words that came in via Norman French. (An interesting exception is the word *law* itself, which comes by way of Old Norse from an Indo-European root word meaning "lay." Law is something "laid down."

With the Renaissance, however, more Latin arrived, words newly coined from the old writings. Some of these were delicately sauced with English pronunciation; others were swallowed whole. The legal profession still clings to its Latin phrases, and still in their original form. Legal documents would be considerably less imposing without the usual sprinkling of words such as *ad hoc, modus vivendi, res justae, habeas corpus, prima facie,* ad infinitum—ad nauseam! As you can see, some even escaped legal bondage.

The new Latin also gave us a host of prefixes and suffixes which added further flexibility to English, though this was a development which occurred somewhat after the Renaissance. What would we do without *ex-, anti-, pro-,* or *-ive, -ism, -ide?* It must be recognized that many of the suffixes, especially, are as much Greek as Latin, and both are part of the new impetus to learning that started with the Renaissance.

All the while that foreign words and phrases were building up our language cake, the whole structure of English was changing, too. The usual Indo-European practice in grammar is to start with a root word and add endings to change the meaning. English grammar, however, has been getting simpler all the time. Nowadays we seldom use endings (except for the possessive *'s,* the plural *s,* and the past-tense and participial endings *-ed* and *-ing.*) Instead we use lots of little helping words to change the meaning. (I dance, I am going to dance, I will have danced.)

It is a lucky thing that our grammar is getting simpler, for our spelling is getting harder all the time. We have, in fact, one of the world's biggest spelling problems. Often our words are not spelled the way they are pronounced, and there is no move toward consistency in sight. Take the matter of *ou,* for example. It is not the same *ou* in "house" as it is in "co*ugh*." And "co*u*sin," "co*u*ld," "thro*ugh*," and "furlo*ugh*" each sport their very own *ou*.

In the matter of making plurals, we run into the same sort of difficulty. When we were children, we used to singsong a little verse about plurals.

> If a mouse and a mouse make mice,
> Why don't
> A house and a house make hice?
>
> If a goose and a goose make geese,
> Why don't
> A moose and a moose make meese?

It still seems a legitimate question.

Apparently all our troubles in English (as well as our very many advantages) stem from our willingness to borrow. When we took foreign words into our language, we took their spelling, too, often their plurals, and always a little something of their pronunciation. That is what makes rules so hard to apply in English. Each word and its spelling is pretty much a law unto itself, and one just has to learn it as best he can.

The borrowing has not stopped, of course. American English has appropriated a host of Spanish and Indian words which bypassed the King's English altogether: *ranch, remuda, rodeo,* for example, and *tomahawk, succotash,* and *hominy.* Then there are the parade of place names, evocative of other times and other peoples. There are Manhattan, Kentucky, Texas, and San Francisco, Los Angeles, and Brazos. That last is short for Brazos de Dios, which name commemorates the feat of a nonswimming friar who, chased by angry savages, plowed through a river "in the arms of God."

The newest layer of American English is being baked with a leavening of teen-age terms and technical terms and slang. "The Apple" is an insider's name for New York. *Nuclear* is out of the laboratory and into the language for fair. *Neat* and *cool* have certainly taken on meanings quite beyond the original *tidy* and *chilly*. And a man who takes a "trip" these days may not necessarily go anywhere in particular.

If English imports words in such great quantity, does it engage in export as well? Yes, certainly, in an ever-growing volume. Technical words go out from America and England with every new invention. American brand names have become household words the world over. Everybody, it seems, drinks Coca-Cola. Beyond that, there is no guarantee. Nobody can say just what words will travel well. The ones that do travel and take hold in other languages may not be to the general liking here.

In Russia, hip teen-agers say, "Okay," refer to wide-brimmed hats as "cowboys," call each other "zhentlemen," and long to do the frug. Even the staid establishment, which frowns on this sort of borrowing, calls its juvenile delinquents "khuligans," from the English word which commemorates forever the spectacular rowdiness of an Irish family named Hooligan.

In Latin America people watch "beisbol" and yell for "jonrons" (home runs). In France *tuer l'arbitre!* still means "kill the umpire!" even if it is in translation. Wherever people drink Coca-Cola, they also eat "hot-dogs." Women everywhere speak of nylons and cold cream, even if they are spelled "nailon" and "colcrem." Japan makes *pikeniku* out of our *picnic,* and has cowboy clubs which practice the "fast draw." And if you have never heard a Japanese rock-and-roller sing in Japanese with an American southern accent, you've missed the ultimate in the borrowing process.

Wherever our fads go, there goes English. But in the long run what goes out is less important than what comes in. The English language—no less than crossroads England herself—preserves a capsule history of

Europe, of its invaders and of their settling down, of internal changes in culture and in the structure of society. The flexibility of English, its willingness to borrow and to add, guarantees that new language layers are yet to be baked. English words will continue to record in themselves great historical changes, great movements still to come. For the West must change or it will diminish, must advance or must retreat. Advance where? Inward into a new world of human understanding; outward again toward the seas of night, uncharted, unknown, where other worlds wait.

TIME	WESTERN EUROPE	ITALY	EASTERN AND CENTRAL EUROPE	AEGEAN	BLACK SEA STEPPES	EGYPT
3500	Mesolithic cultures in Britain		Long-house settlements Mound villages			Neolithic cultures
	Spain colonized—from the Aegean(?)					
3000	Farming in Britain				Domestication of horse	Two lands united in one kingdom
	Collective earthen tombs in Britain Rock-cut temples and tombs in Malta		Swiss Lake Dwellers	Early Minoan civilization Big rowing boats	Mound burials	Old Kingdom (Dynasties 1–6)
					Battle-ax People move west	
2500	Outer circle at Stonehenge				Pastoral societies on Black Sea coast	
			Battle-ax burials and log roads	Destruction on mainland—Luwians(?)		End of Old Kingdom
	Beaker Folk on the move British trade in metals					
2000			End of mound villages			Middle Kingdom
	Beaker Folk and Battle-ax People mingle		Beaker Folk and Battle-ax People mingle	Middle Minoan palace building on Crete		
	Beaker Folk in Britain					
				Arrival of Greeks(?)	Ancestral Scythians(?)	End of Middle Kingdom; Hyksos
				New dynasty at Mycenae Shaft graves, horses and chariots		Hyksos expelled New Kingdom Thutmose I
1500	Inner Stonehenge circle European High Bronze Age			Knossos sacked		Hatshepsut Thutmose III Thutmose IV
			Burial rites change (cremation) with Urnfield expansion			
		Urnfield culture				Rameses II
	Urnfield culture in Britain	Earliest Roman settlement	Hallstatt Culture (use of iron)	Trojan War(?) Dorians(?)	Riding astride(?)	Rameses III fights Sea People
1000	Hallstatt Culture	Hallstatt Culture	Scythians(?)		Scythians moving west(?)	
		Etruscan cities		Phoenician script brought to Greece		
	Celts in Britain	Greek colonies Legendary founding of Rome		Homer First Olympiad	Massagetae	Assyrians
500	High Celtic period	The Roman Republic	High Celtic period			Persians
		Celts threaten Rome		Socrates, Pericles		
		Rome conquers rest of Italy	Teutonic tribes grow strong	Athens defeated by Sparta Alexander Conquest of Persia	Sarmatians displace Scythians	Alexander Under Greek Ptolemies
				Roman conquest of Greece	Huns defeat Massagetae	
B.C.	Caesar conquers Celts	Roman Empire established	Celts pushed west			Annexed by Rome
A.D.	Romans conquer Britain	Height of Roman Empire	Goths move south		Huns move west	
			Goths enter Roman Dacia			
		Sarmatian campaigns				
	Frankish break-through Huns in Gaul Franks defeat Romans	Decline of Empire Visigoths plunder Rome			Huns	
500	Anglo-Saxons in Britain	Huns and Vandals	Huns break Ostrogoths, arrive in Hungary	Slavs		

SYRO-PALESTINE	ANATOLIA	CAUCASIAN STEPPES	MESOPOTAMIA	PERSIA	INDIA	TIME
...o and other ...led towns long ...xistence	Town life already old (Catal Hüyük)		Arrival of Sumerians(?) Cities; first writing			3500
	Troy I	Domestication of horse(?)				3000
		Mound burials	Royal cemeteries at Ur			
	Troy II, Alaca Hüyük	Battle-ax People moving west Mound burials	Struggles among Sumerian cities		Beginning of Indus civilization(?)	2500
...rite raids	Troy II falls; Luwians(?)	Solid-wheeled wooden carts and clay models in burials	Sargon, king of Akkad Indus seal stones in Lagash Gutians overrun Sumer Amorite raids			
...ians move in	Hittites(?)		Assyria independent			2000
			Horse mentioned in Sumerian literature			
...e-ax People(?)	Siege of Hattusas by Hittites Hattusilis I		Hammurabi's dynasty			
...of Mitanni		Aryans move out(?)				
...tians dominant	Telipinus (first annals)		Kassite conquest			1500
...i dominant over ...tanni	Iron smelting a Hittite secret				Arrival of Aryans(?) Downfall of Indus civilization	
...le of Kadesh ...ria absorbs ...itanni ...of Hebrews	Phrygians overrun Hatti Greek refugees in Ionian cities	Riding astride Medes and Persians move out	Kassites overthrown, return to Luristan			1000
...of Phoenician ...ies	New Hittite kingdoms	Cimmerians	Assyrian empire Babylonian kingdom revived	Medes and Persians	Immigrations into Ganges basin Cities in Ganges basin	
	Cimmerian invasion Phrygians replaced by Lydian kingdom	Massagetae dominant	Assyria falls Babylon falls	Medes defeat Assyria Zoroaster(?) Cyrus Babylon falls to Cyrus	Large kingdoms in northeast The forest sages Buddha	500
				Darius attacks Greece		
...er Seleucid or ...olemaic rule	Kingdom of Pontus	Huns defeat Massagetae	Seleucid rule	Alexander conquers Persia Persia ruled by Greeks Parthian revolt Parthian empire	Alexander's invasion Ashoka	
...nexed by Rome	Annexed by Rome			Parthians defeat Romans	Scythians in India	B.C.
...s of Nazareth	Sarmatian invasions	Sarmatians invade Parthia		Sarmatians invade	Kushon dynasty	A.D.
	Roman imperial capital moved to Byzantium			Persia under Sassanian rule	Huns in India	
	Justinian			Struggles between Persia and Rome Peace with Justinian		500

Bibliography

PROLOGUE

Campbell, Joseph, *The Masks of God: Occidental Mythology*. New York: The Viking Press, Inc., 1964.

Childe, Vere Gordon, *The Aryans: A Study of Indo-European Origins*. New York: Alfred A. Knopf, Inc., 1926.

——————————, *The Dawn of European Civilization*. New York: Alfred A. Knopf, Inc., 1958.

Gimbutas, Marja, "Indo-Europeans: Archaeological Problem." *American Anthropologist,* Vol. 65, No. 4 (1963), pp. 815–36.

Haskins, John F., "The Royal Scythians." *Natural History Magazine* (October, 1960), pp. 8–18.

Hencken, Hugh, *Indo-European Languages and Archaeology*. American Anthropological Association, Memoir #84, Vol. 57, No. 6 (December, 1955).

Hudson, Alfred E., *Kazak Social Structure*. Yale University Publications in Anthropology #20. New Haven: Yale University Press, 1938.

Partridge, Eric, *Origins*. New York: The Macmillan Company, 1961.

Pei, Mario, *Families of Words*. New York: Harper & Row, Publishers, 1962.

——————————, "Language's Curious Couples." *Saturday Review of Literature* (December 3, 1960).

——————————, *The Story of Language*. New York: Mentor Books, 1949.

Phillips, E. D., "Nomad Peoples of the Steppes," in S. Piggott, ed., *Dawn of Civilization* (New York: McGraw-Hill Book Company, Inc., 1961).

Piggott, Stuart, *Ancient Europe*. Chicago: Aldine Publishing Company, 1965.

——————————, "The Beginnings of Wheel Transport." *Scientific American* (July, 1968).

Rice, Tamara Talbot, *The Scythians*. New York: Frederick A. Praeger, Inc., 1957.

Ross, A. S. C., *Etymology*. London: Oxford University Press, 1958.

Trager, George L., "Languages of the World," in *Collier's Encyclopedia* (New York: Crowell, Collier and Macmillan, Inc., 1965).

CHAPTER I

Adams, Robert M., "The Origin of Cities." *Scientific American* (September, 1960).

Chiera, Walter, *They Wrote on Clay*. Chicago: University of Chicago Press, 1938.

Childe, Vere Gordon, *Man Makes Himself*. New York: New American Library of World Literature, Inc., 1951.

——————————, *New Light on the Most Ancient East*. London: Kegan Paul, Trench, Trubner & Company, Ltd., 1934.

Culican, William, *The Medes and Persians*. New York: Frederick A. Praeger, Inc., 1965.

Gadd, C. J., *The Dynasty of Agade and the Gutian Invasion*. Cambridge Ancient History. Cambridge: Cambridge University Press, 1963.

Goldman, Bernard, "The Bronzes of Luristan." *Natural History Magazine* (May, 1964), pp. 12–21.

Jacobsen, Thorkild, "Mesopotamia," in H. and H. A. Frankfort, eds., *Before Philosophy* (Middlesex, G. B.: Penguin Books, Ltd., 1959).

Kramer, Samuel Noah, *History Begins at Sumer*. Garden City, N.Y.: Doubleday & Company, Inc., 1959.

——————————, *The Sumerians*. Chicago: University of Chicago Press, 1963.

Malowan, M. E., "The Birth of Written History," in S. Piggott, ed., *Dawn of Civilization* (New York: McGraw-Hill Book Company, Inc., 1961).

Oppenheim, A. Leo, *Ancient Mesopotamia*. Chicago: University of Chicago Press, 1964.

Phillips, E. D., "The Vanished Cultures of Luristan, Mannai, and Urartu," in E. Bacon, ed., *Vanished Civilizations of the Ancient World* (New York: McGraw-Hill Book Company, Inc., 1963).

Woolley, Sir Leonard, *The Development of Sumerian Art*. New York: Charles Scribner's Sons, 1935.

——————————, *Excavations at Ur,* 2nd ed. New York: Barnes & Noble, Inc., 1963.

——————————, *The Sumerians*. Oxford: The Clarendon Press, 1929.

Woolley, Sir Leonard, and Hawkes, Jacquetta, *Prehistory and the Beginnings of Civilization*. New York: Harper & Row, Publishers, 1963.

CHAPTER 2

Akurgal, Ekrem, *The Art of the Hittites.* New York: Harry N. Abrams, Inc., Publishers, 1962.

Blegan, Carl W., *Troy.* Cambridge Ancient History. Cambridge: Cambridge University Press, 1961.

Gurney, O. R., *The Hittites,* rev. ed. Baltimore: Penguin Books, 1964.

Hencken, Hugh, *Indo-European Languages and Archaeology.* American Anthropological Association, Memoir #84, Vol. 57, No. 6 (December, 1955).

Lloyd, Seton, "The Early Settlement of Anatolia," in S. Piggott, ed., *Dawn of Civilization* (New York: McGraw-Hill Book Company, Inc., 1961).

Mellaart, James, *Anatolia, c. 4000–2300 B.C.* Cambridge Ancient History. Cambridge: Cambridge University Press, 1962.

————————, *Catal Hüyük.* New York: McGraw-Hill Book Company, Inc., 1967.

————————, *Earliest Civilizations of the Near East.* New York: McGraw-Hill Book Company, Inc., 1965.

Porada, Edith, "Ancient Hatti." *Natural History Magazine* (June–July, 1959), pp. 308–20.

Reference Notes

The quotation on pages 58 and 59 are from Gurney, *The Hittites.*
The second quotation on page 59 is cited by Akurgal in *The Art of the Hittites.*

CHAPTER 3

Albright, W. F., *The Archaeology of Palestine,* rev. ed. Baltimore: Penguin Books, 1961.

————————, "Mitannian Maryannu, 'Chariot Warrior,' and the Canaanite and Egyptian Equivalents," *Archiv für Orientforschung,* VI (1930), p. 217.

Anati, Emmanuel, *Palestine Before the Hebrews.* New York: Alfred A. Knopf, Inc., 1963.

Culican, William, "Sea People of the Levant," in S. Piggott, ed., *Dawn of Civilization* (New York: McGraw-Hill Book Company, Inc., 1961).

Gurney, O. R., *The Hittites,* rev. ed. Baltimore: Penguin Books, 1964.

Kupper, J. R., *Northern Mesopotamia and Syria.* Cambridge Ancient History. Cambridge: Cambridge University Press.

Meek, Theophile James, *Hebrew Origins.* New York: Harper & Row, Publishers, 1960.

Moscati, Sabatino, *Ancient Semitic Civilizations.* New York: G. P. Putnam's Sons, 1957.

Thieme, Paul, "The 'Aryan' Gods of the Mitanni Treaties." *Proceedings of the American Oriental Society,* 80 (1960), pp. 301–17.

Wilson, John A., *The Culture of Ancient Egypt.* Chicago: University of Chicago Press, 1951.

Woolley, Sir Leonard, *A Forgotten Kingdom.* Baltimore: Penguin Books, 1953.

CHAPTER 4

Albright, W. F., *The Archaeology of Palestine,* rev. ed. Baltimore: Penguin Books, 1961.

——————————————, "Mitannian Maryannu, 'Chariot Warrior,' and the Canaanite and Egyptian Equivalents." *Archiv für Orientforschung,* VI (1930), p. 217.

Aldred, Cyril, "The Rise of the God Kings," in S. Piggott, ed., *Dawn of Civilization.* (New York: McGraw-Hill Book Company, Inc., 1961).

Anati, Emmanuel, *Palestine Before the Hebrews.* New York: Alfred A. Knopf, Inc., 1963.

Breasted, J. H., *Development of Religion and Thought in Ancient Egypt.* New York: Harper & Row, Publishers, 1959.

——————————————, *A History of Egypt from Earliest Times to the Persian Conflict.* New York: Charles Scribner's Sons, 1909.

Childe, Vere Gordon, *What Happened in History.* Baltimore: Penguin Books, 1946.

Glanville, S. R. K., ed., *The Legacy of Egypt.* Oxford: The Clarendon Press, 1942.

Säve-Söderbergh, T., "The Hyksos Rule in Egypt." *Journal of Egyptian Archaeology,* XXXVII (1951), pp. 53–71.

Wilson, John A., *The Culture of Ancient Egypt.* Chicago: University of Chicago Press, 1951.

——————————————, "Egypt," in H. and H. A. Frankfort, eds., *Before Philosophy* (Middlesex, G. B.: Penguin Books, Ltd., 1959).

Reference Notes

The quotation on page 76 is from Breasted, *Development of Religion and Thought in Ancient Egypt.*

The quotation on page 77 is from Wilson, *The Culture of Ancient Egypt.*

The quotation on page 79 is from Säve-Söderbergh, "The Hyksos Rule in Egypt."

The comparison on page 85 is cited by W. O. E. Oesterley in Glanville, ed., *The Legacy of Egypt.*

The comparison on page 86 is from Breasted, *A History of Egypt from Earliest Times to the Persian Conflict.*

CHAPTER 5

Bacon, Edward, "Bridge to the Ancient East," in E. Bacon, ed., *Vanished Civilizations of the Ancient World* (New York: McGraw-Hill Book Company, Inc., 1963).

Campbell, Joseph, *The Masks of God: Oriental Mythology.* New York: The Viking Press, Inc., 1959.

Coon, Carleton S., *The Living Races of Man.* New York: Alfred A. Knopf, Inc., 1965.

Dales, George F., "The Decline of the Harappans." *Scientific American* (May, 1966).

Fairservis, Walter A., Jr., "The Chronology of the Harappan Civilization and the Aryan Invasions." *Man,* Vol. LVI, Article 173 (1956).

Frye, Richard N., *The Heritage of Persia.* Cleveland: World Publishing Company, 1963.

Heine-Geldern, Robert, "The Coming of the Aryans and the End of Harappan Civilization." *Man,* Vol. LVI, Article 151 (1956).

Kosambi, D. D., *Ancient India.* New York: Pantheon Books, Inc., 1965.

——————————, "Living Prehistory in India." *Scientific American* (February, 1967).

Larousse Encyclopedia of Mythology. New York: Prometheus Press, 1959.

Raikes, Robert L., "The End of the Ancient Cities of the Indus." *American Anthropologist* (April, 1964), pp. 284–300.

Thieme, Paul, "The 'Aryan' Gods of the Mitanni Treaties." *Proceedings of the American Oriental Society,* 80 (1960), pp. 301–17.

Thomas, Edward J., *Vedic Hymns.* New York: E. P. Dutton & Company, Inc., 1923.

Wheeler, Sir Mortimer, *Civilizations of the Indus Valley and Beyond.* New York: McGraw-Hill Book Company, Inc., 1966.

——————————, *Early India and Pakistan.* New York: Frederick A. Praeger, Inc., 1959.

Woolley, Sir Leonard, and Hawkes, Jacquetta, *Prehistory and the Beginnings of Civilization.* New York: Harper & Row, Publishers, 1963.

Reference Notes

The quotation on page 90 is from Frye, *The Heritage of Persia.*
The quotations on page 91 are from Thomas, *Vedic Hymns.*

CHAPTER 6

Culican, William, *The Medes and Persians*. New York: Frederick A. Praeger, Inc., 1965.

Duchesne-Guillermin, Jacques, *Symbols and Values in Zoroastrianism*. New York: Harper & Row, Publishers, 1966.

Frye, Richard N., *The Heritage of Persia*. Cleveland: World Publishing Company, 1963.

Ghirshman, Roman, *The Arts of Ancient Iran,* trans. by S. Gilbert and J. Emmons. New York: Golden Press, Inc., 1964.

Herodotus, *The Histories,* trans. by Harry Carter. New York: The Heritage Press, 1958.

Oates, David, "The Rise and Fall of Sassanian Iran," in David Talbot Rice, ed., *Dawn of European Civilization* (New York: McGraw-Hill Book Company, Inc., 1965).

Zaehner, R. C., *The Dawn and Twilight of Zoroastrianism*. New York: G. P. Putnam's Sons, 1961.

Reference Notes

The quotation on page 110 is from Herodotus, *The Histories,* translated by Carter.

The quotation on page 113 is from the foundation texts uncovered at Susa, as cited by Culican in *The Medes and Persians*.

CHAPTER 7

Bibby, Geoffrey, "Before the Argo." *Horizon,* Vol. II, No. 6 (1960).

Bowra, C. M., "Homer's Age of Heroes." *Horizon,* Vol. III, No. 3 (1961).

Chadwick, John, *The Decipherment of Linear B. Natural History Magazine* (March–April, 1961).

——————————————, *The Prehistory of the Greek Language*. Cambridge Ancient History. Cambridge: Cambridge University Press, 1963.

Evans, Sir Arthur, *The Ring of Nestor*. London: MacMillan Company, Ltd., 1925.

Harrison, Jane Ellen, *Prolegomena to the Study of Greek Religion*. Cambridge: Cambridge University Press, 1922.

Homer, *The Iliad,* trans. by W. H. D. Rouse. New York: New American Library, 1954.

Hood, M. S. F., "The Aegean Before the Greeks," in S. Piggott, ed., *Dawn of Civilization* (New York: McGraw-Hill Book Company, Inc., 1961).

Huxley, George, "The History Which Inspired Homer," in M. Grant, ed., *Birth of Western Civilization* (McGraw-Hill Book Company, Inc., 1964).

Matz, F., *Minoan Civilization: Maturity and Zenith*. Cambridge Ancient History. Cambridge: Cambridge University Press, 1962.

Mellaart, James, *Anatolia, c. 4000–2300* B.C. Cambridge Ancient History. Cambridge: Cambridge University Press, 1962.

Palmer, Leonard R., *Mycenaeans and Minoans*. New York: Alfred A. Knopf, Inc., 1963.

Piggott, Stuart, *Ancient Europe*. Chicago: Aldine Publishing Company, 1965.

Reverdin, Olivier, *Crete and Its Treasures*. New York: The Viking Press, Inc., 1961.

Stubbings, Frank H., *The Rise of Mycenaean Civilization*. Cambridge Ancient History. Cambridge: Cambridge University Press, 1963.

CHAPTER 8

Campbell, Joseph, *The Masks of God: Occidental Mythology*. New York: The Viking Press, Inc., 1964.

Durant, Will, *The Life of Greece*. New York: Simon and Schuster, Inc., 1939.

Fitts, Dudley, *Greek Plays in Translation*. New York: The Dial Press, Inc., 1947.

Hamilton, Edith, *The Echo of Greece*. New York: W. W. Norton & Company, Inc., 1957.

————————————, *The Greek Way*. New York: W. W. Norton & Company, Inc., 1942.

Herodotus, *The Histories,* trans. by Harry Carter. New York: The Heritage Press, 1958.

Jowett, B., ed., *Works of Plato*. New York: The Dial Press, Inc.

Livingstone, R. W., *The Legacy of Greece*. Oxford: The Clarendon Press, 1921.

McKeon, R., *Introduction to Aristotle*. New York: Modern Library, Inc., 1947.

Muller, Herbert J., *The Loom of History*. New York: Harper and Row, Publishers, 1958.

————————————, *The Uses of the Past*. New York: New American Library, Inc., 1954.

Mylonas, George E., *Eleusis and the Eleusinian Mysteries*. Princeton: Princeton University Press, 1961.

Robinson, C. A., Jr., "The Two Worlds of Alexander." *Horizon,* Vol. I, No. 4 (1959).

Toynbee, Arnold, *Greek Civilization and Character*. New York: New American Library, Inc., 1953.

————————, *Greek Historical Thought*. New York: New American Library, Inc., 1952.

Reference Notes

The quotation on page 138 is from Mylonas, *Eleusis and the Eleusinian Mysteries.*

The quotation on page 147 is from Robinson, "The Two Worlds of Alexander."

CHAPTER 9

Bailey, Cyril, ed., *The Legacy of Rome*. Oxford: The Clarendon Press, 1924.

Barrow, R. H., *The Romans*. Middlesex, G. B.: Penguin Books, Ltd., 1949.

Bloch, Raymond, "In Search of the Etruscans." *Horizon*, Vol. II, No. 5 (1960).

Caesar, Julius, *The Gallic Wars*, trans. by John Warrington. New York: The Heritage Press, 1955.

Campbell, Joseph, *The Masks of God: Occidental Mythology*. New York: The Viking Press, Inc., 1964.

Childe, Vere Gordon, *Prehistoric Migrations in Europe*. Cambridge: Harvard University Press, 1950.

Durant, Will, *Caesar and Christ*. New York: Simon and Schuster, Inc., 1944.

Goad, Harold, *Language in History*. London: Penguin Books, Ltd., 1958.

Hadas, Moses, *A History of Rome from Its Origins to 529 A.D. As Told by the Roman Historians*. Garden City, N.Y.: Doubleday & Company, Inc., 1956.

Hamilton, Edith, *The Roman Way*. New York: New American Library, Inc., 1957.

Muller, Herbert J., *The Uses of the Past*. New York: New American Library, 1954.

Piggott, Stuart, *Ancient Europe*. Chicago: Aldine Publishing Company, 1965.

Suetonius, *The Twelve Caesars*, trans. by Robert Graves. Baltimore: Penguin Books, 1957.

Reference Note

The quotation on page 159 is from Hadas, *A History of Rome from Its Origins to 529 A.D. As Told by the Roman Historians.*

CHAPTER 10

Caesar, Julius, *The Gallic Wars*, trans. by John Warrington. New York: The Heritage Press, 1955.

Campbell, Joseph, *The Masks of God: Occidental Mythology.* New York: The Viking Press, Inc., 1964.

Daniel, Glyn E., "Megaliths and Men." *Natural History Magazine* (April, 1963).

Hencken, Hugh, *Indo-European Languages and Archaeology.* American Anthropological Association, Memoir #84, Vol. 57, No. 6 (December, 1955).

Piggott, Stuart, *Ancient Europe.* Chicago: Aldine Publishing Company, 1965.

Powell, T. G. E., "From the First Farmers to the Celts," in S. Piggott, ed., *Dawn of Civilization* (New York: McGraw-Hill Book Company, Inc., 1961).

Ross, Anne, *Pagan Celtic Britain.* New York: Columbia University Press, 1967.

Sieveking, Gale, "The Migration of the Megaliths," in E. Bacon, ed., *Vanished Civilizations of the Ancient World* (New York: McGraw-Hill Book Company, Inc., 1963).

Tacitus, *Complete Works,* trans. by Alfred John Church and William Jackson Brodribb. New York: Modern Library, Inc., 1942.

Reference Note

The quotations on pages 173, 174, and 175 are from Caesar's *The Gallic Wars,* translated by John Warrington.

CHAPTER 11

Bullough, Donald, "The Ostrogothic and Lombard Kingdoms," in David Talbot Rice, ed., *Dawn of European Civilization* (New York: McGraw-Hill Book Company, Inc., 1965).

Caesar, Julius, *The Gallic Wars,* trans. by John Warrington. New York: The Heritage Press, 1955.

Culican, William, "The Ends of the Earth," in *Dawn of European Civilization.*

Durant, Will, *The Age of Faith.* New York: Simon and Schuster, Inc., 1950.

Gibbon, Edward. *The Decline and Fall of the Roman Empire.* New York: The Heritage Press, 1946.

Lasko, Peter, "Prelude to Empire," in *Dawn of European Civilization.*

Oxenstierna, Eric, "The Vikings." *Scientific American* (May, 1967).

Phillips, E. D., "Nomad Peoples of the Steppes," in S. Piggott, ed., *Dawn of Civilization* (New York: McGraw-Hill Book Company, Inc., 1961).

Rice, Tamara Talbot, "Eastern Europe and the Rise of the Slavs," in *Dawn of European Civilization.*

——————————, *The Scythians.* New York: Frederick A. Praeger, Inc., 1957.

Sulimirski, T., "The Forgotten Sarmatians," in E. Bacon, ed., *Vanished Civili-*

zations of the Ancient World (New York: McGraw-Hill Book Company, Inc., 1963).

Tacitus, *Complete Works,* trans. by Alfred John Church and William Jackson Brodribb. New York: Modern Library, Inc., 1942.

Wilson, David M., "The Norsemen and Their Forerunners," in *Dawn of European Civilization.*

Reference Notes

The quotations on pages 182, 190, 191, and 193 are from Tacitus, *Complete Works,* translated by Church and Brodribb.

The translation on page 189 is by J. Martin, as cited in Rice, *The Scythians.*

Epilogue

Beowulf, trans. by William Ellery Leonard. New York: The Heritage Press, 1939.

Clark, Grahame, *Prehistoric England.* London: B. T. Batsford, Ltd., 1961.

Hawkes, Jacquetta and Christopher, *Prehistoric Britain.* London: Chatto & Windus, Ltd., 1962.

Hawkins, Gerald S., and White, J. B., *Stonehenge Decoded.* Garden City, N.Y.: Doubleday & Company, Inc., 1965.

Hencken, Hugh, *Indo-European Languages and Archaeology.* American Anthropological Association, Memoir #84, Vol. 57, No. 6 (December, 1955).

Jesperson, Otto, *Growth and Structure of the English Language.* Oxford: Basil Blackwell, 1948.

Pei, Mario, *The Story of Language.* New York: Mentor Books, 1949.

Piggott, Stuart, *Ancient Europe.* Chicago: Aldine Publishing Company, 1965.

Salisbury, Harrison, Articles on the Soviet Union in *The New York Times* (February, 1962).

Sieveking, Gale, "The Migration of the Megaliths," in E. Bacon, ed., *Vanished Civilizations of the Ancient World* (New York: McGraw-Hill Book Company, Inc., 1963).

Trevelyan, G. M., *History of England,* Vol. 1. Garden City, N.Y.: Doubleday & Company, Inc., 1953.

Index

Page numbers in italics refer to maps and charts.

Achaeans, 19, *19*, 22, 124, 125, 128–32
Aegean Sea, 22, *124*
Aeschylus, 145
Afghanistan, 89, 93, *94*
Ahuramazda, 106–07, 108, 112, 113, 115
Akhetaton, *78*, 82
Akhnaton, 80, 81–82, 85
Akkadian language, 35, 42, 43
Alaca Hüyük, *49*, 51
Albright, W. F., 62
Aleppo, *65*, 69
Alexander of Macedon, 71, 84, 100, 114, 146–47, 173
Alexandria, *78*, 86
Algebra, invention of, 101
Alphabet, invention of, 67
Alps, *12*, *151*, 152, 153, 168, 173
Amazons, origin of myth of, 27
Amorites, 43, 63, 64
Anatolia, *12*, 18, 22, 32, 42, 47–59, *49*, *65*, 114, 115, 122–23, 124, 131, 133, *141*, 143, 166, 171, 173
Anaximander, 136
Anglo-Saxons, 190, 198, 199; language of, 24, *25*, 199–200, *200*
Arabia, 61, 101, 117, *157*
Ares, 16, 128
Aristarchus, 136
Aristotle, 146
Armenia, 61, *109*, *157*
Armenian language, 23, *25*, 33
Aryans, *19*, 89–90, 91, 95, 96, 97, 98, 99;

India invaded by, *19*, 35, 71, 89, 90, 91–92, *94*, 95, 103
Ashoka, 101
Assur, *34*, 112
Assurbanipal, King, 45
Assyria, *34*, 42, 43, 44, 45, 56, 59, 68, 70, 84, 107, 108, *109*
Astyages, King, 107–08, 110
Aswan Dam, 83
Athena, 128, 138
Athens, *124*, 133, 135, 138, 141, *141*, 142, 143, 144, 145–46
Aton, 82, 85, 86
Attila, 186, 187
Augustus (Octavian), 156, 182

Babylon, *34*, 35, 36, 43, 44, 68, 107, 108, 110, 113, 143
Babylonia, 18, 35, 36, 38, 39, 43, 44, 45, 52, 55, 108, *109*
Bactria, 107, *109*, 147
Baltic Sea, *12*, 185, 192
Battle-ax People, 24, 26–28, 61, 66, 68, 77, 168; graves of, 15–16, 18, 27; as herdsmen, 26; metallurgy of, 24; migrations of, 17–20, *19*, 32–35, 50, 128; and trade with Sumerians, 17
Bell Beaker Folk, 168, 196, 197
Benares, *94*, 98
Bible, Judeo-Christian, 38, 63, 64
Black Sea, *12*, 18, *19*, 22, 47, *49*, 50, 56, 92, *109*, 131, *141*, 142, 184, 185, 192

Brahma, 99, 102
Brahmā, 102, 103
Brahmans, 96–97, 98, 99, 102, 106
Britain, 14, 22, 156, *157*, 172, 173, 174, 190, 194–99
Buddha, 99–100, 101, 102, 105
Bull, in ancient Crete, 126
Byblos, 61, *65*, 67, 71
Byzantium, 117

Caesar, Julius, 156, 157, 173, 174, 175, 176, 181, 198
Calendar, 161–62
Cambyses, 111
Campbell, Joseph, 93
Carpathian Mountains, *12*, 14, 168
Carthage, 151, *151*, 152, 153, 154
Caspian Sea, *12, 19, 34*, 106, *109*, 192
Catal Hüyük, 48–50, *49*
Caucasic languages, 33
Caucasus Mountains, *12*, 15, 17, 18, 19, *19*, 20, 32, 33, 34, *34*, 47, *49*, 50, 90, 107, *109*
Celtic languages, 23, 24, 25, 172, 197–98
Celts, *19*, 20, 22, 71, *151*, 172–77, 180, 182, 197, 198
China, 14, 36, *94*, 101, 114, 117, 189
Christianity, 64, 86, 87, 110, 163
Cicero, 150, 154, 158
Cisalpine Gaul, 154, *157*
Cleopatra, 84
Confucius, 105
Copper smelting, 48
Corinth, 122, *124, 141*, 142
Crete, 121, 122–28, *124*, 129, 130, 132, 133, 138
Croesus, King, 143
Cuneiform writing, 37, 51–52
Cyrus the Great, 108, 110, 111, 143

Dacia, *157*, 184, 185
Danube River, *12*, 14, 22, 165, 166, *170*
Darius I, 111, 112, 113, 143

Darius III, 146
Delhi, *94*, 98
Delphi, *170*, 173
Democritus, 136
Dorians, *19*, 22, 132, 133, 142, 152
Druids, 175, 176

Egypt, 18, 22, 55, 56, *65*, 66–70 *passim*, 73–76, 77, *78*, 79–87, *109*, 130, *157*; religion of, 76, 84–86
Elam, *34*, 43
Electra, 138
Elephantine, *78*, 79
Eleusinian rites, 138
Eleusis, 138, *141*
English language, 24, *25*, 161, 194–95, 200–05
Eridu, *34*, 36
Ertha, 181–82
Etruscans, 150–51, *151*, 153
Euphrates River, *12*, 17, *19*, 33, *34*, 36, 47, *49*, 65, 66, 69, *109*
Euripides, 145
Evans, Sir Arthur, 132

Flood, Sumerian story of, 39–40
Franks, 185

Galatia, *157*, 173
Ganges system, *94*, 98
Gaul, 22, *151*, 156, *157*, 173, 174, 190, 192
Genghis Khan, 27, 28, 186
Germanic languages, 23, 24, 25
Germans (Teutons), *19*, 22, 179–82, 185, 187, 190–91, 193
Gibbon, Edward, 186
Goths, 182, 185
Gracchi, 155
Graves, 15–16, 18, 27, 51, 131
Greece, 16, 19, 38, 59, 70, *109*, 113, 114, 117, 123, *124*, 130, 131, 133, 135–47, *141*, *151*, 154, *157*, 158, 159, 171

Greek language, 23, 24, *25*, 201
Gutians, *34*, 42, 43

Halicarnassus, 123, *124*
Hallstatt People, *170*, 171–72
Hammurabi, King, 18, 35, 43, 44
Hannibal, 153
Harappa, 94, *94*, 95
Hatshepsut, Queen, 80, 81
Hatti, 51, 52, 53, 55, 56, 70, 71, 82
Hattusas, *49*, 53, 56, 57
Hattusilis I, 53, 58
Hebrews, 22, 38–39, 40, 62, 64, 70, 84, 85, 108
Hellespont, 48, *49*, 50, 56, 59, 114, *124*, 143, 144, 146
Herodotus, 26, 110, 111, 113, 144, 176
Hieroglyphs, Cretan, 124
Hinduism, 102
Hippocrates, 137
Hittite Empire, *49*, 56, 131
Hittites, 18, *19*, 22, 47, *49*, 51–53, 55–59, 69, 70, 91
Homer, 121, 130, 131, 132, 133, 146
Huns, 184, 185, 186, 187, 190, 192
Hurrians, 64–66, 70; language of, 69
Hyksos, 18, *19*, 66, 71, 76–77, 79, 80, 84, 130

Ice age, last, *12*, 13
Iceland, 193
Iliad, 131
Illyria, *157*
India, 15, 16, 22, 71, 93, *94*, 96, 97, 101, 102, 105, *109*, 118; *see also* Aryans
Indo-European languages, 15, 22–24, *25*, 28, 33, 96, 168, 202
Indra, 16, 69, 90, 91, 95, 98, 102, 103, 106
Indus River, *19*, 92, 94, *94*, 98, *109*
Iran, *12*, 13, 15, 89
Iranian Plateau, *12*, 19, 20, 89, 107
Iron smelting, by Hittites, 54, 55
Isis, 84, 155

Islam, 64, 87, 118
Italy, 19, 152, 153, *157*, 176, 177, 190, 200

Jericho, 48, 62, 63, *65*
Jordanian valley, 61, 62, *65*
Judaism, 109
Juno, 150, 158
Jupiter, 16, 158

Kadesh, *49;* Battle of, 55
Kassites, 18, *19*, *34*, 34–36, 44, 45, 52, 55, 91
Kish, *34*, 42
Knossos, 121, 123, *124*, 125, 129
Konya Plain, *49*, 50
Kosambi, *94*, 98
Krishna, 102
Kukun, Luwian, 66

Labarnas, King, 53
Labyrinth, in Knossos, 121–22
Lagash, *34*, 42, 43
Latin language, 23, 24, *25*, 149–50, 152, 161, 201, 202
Law codes, 37, 41–42, 44, 57–58, 111, 159–60, 163
Lebanon, 61, 62, *65*
Leonidas, King, 144
Linear A, 124, 129
Linear B, 124, 128, 129
Lukka-Man, 66
Luristan, 33, *34*, 112
Luwians, *19*, *49*, 50, 66, 123, 130; language of, 50, 124
Lydia, *109*, *141*, 143

Macedonia, *141*, 146, *157*
Macedonian Wars, 154
Magi, 106, 107, 116
Magna Graecia, 151, *151*
Marathon, Battle of, 143, 144
Marcus Aurelius, *157*, 185, 188
Marduk, 44, 110, 113

Maryannu, 66–71 *passim*, 77, 80
Massagetae, 184
Massilia, *141, 170,* 171
Mauryan Empire, 100, 101
Mazdaism, 107, 110
Medes, 45, 89, 90, 106, 107, 108
Mediterranean Sea, *12,* 47, *49, 65, 78, 109,* 141, *141, 151,* 156
Megaliths, 167
Mesopotamia, 18, 33, *34,* 37, 38, 40, 45, 47, 48, 63, 64, 65, 71, 74, 77, 108, *157,* 192
Middle East, 20, 48, 82, 117, 170, 188; metal trade in, 48; Mitanni in, *65*
Miletus, *124,* 131
Minoans, 121, 125, 132
Minotaur, legend of, 127
Mitanni, 18, *19, 49,* 52, 55, 56, *65,* 68–71, 80, 82
Mithraism, 115–16
Mitra, 16, 69, 91, 97, 106, 110, 192
Mohenjo-Daro, 94, *94,* 95, 103
Mongols, 27, 186
Mycenae, *124,* 130, 131, 133, 138

Nefertiti, Queen, 81
Negev, *65,* 80
Nile River, *12, 19,* 73–74, *78, 109*
Nippur, *34,* 41
Normans, 192, 199; language of, *200*
North Africa, 153

Odin, 181
Odyssey, 131
Oedipus, 138
Olympic Games, 139, 142
Osiris, 76
Ostrogoths, 185, 188, 190

Pakistan, 33, 92, 93, *94*
Pala people, *49,* 50
Palestine, 56, 62, 64, 67, 68, 69, 76, 77, *78,* 80

Palmer, Leonard, 124
Parnassos, 123
Pars, *109,* 116
Parsees, 118
Parthia, *109,* 114–15, 116, 117
Pax Romana, 158
Peloponnese, *124,* 133
Peloponnesian War, 140
Pericles, 135, 141, 145
Persian Empire, *109,* 110, 114, 117, 143, 147
Persian Gulf, 17, *34,* 36, 107, *109*
Persians, *19,* 35, 45, 59, 84, 89, 90, 91, 105, 106, 107, 108, 111, 114, 118, 143; and Greeks, 143–45; language of, *25, 33,* 118; religion of, 110, 116–17
Pharaoh, 74–75
Philip of Macedon, 146
Philistines, 56, 70
Phoenicians, 133, 142
Phrygians, *19,* 22, 56, 59, 152
Piggott, Stuart, 177
Plataea, Battle of, 144
Plato, 146, 158
Poseidon, 16, 128, 158
Pottery, 48, 93
Proto-Romans, 19, *19*
Pylos, *124,* 132
Pyramids, Egyptian, 75
Pyrrhus, King, 153

Rameses II, 80, 83
Ravi River, 94, *94*
Religion, 16, 20, 76, 84, 90–91, 99–110 *passim,* 115–17, 126, 138, 158, 175, 176–77, 181–82
Rhine River, 182, 185
Rhone River, 167, *170*
Roman Catholic Church, 163, 191
Roman Empire, 154, 155–60, *157,* 183, 184; invaded by barbarians, 162, 187, 188

Roman Republic, 154, 158, 160, 193
Romans, 22, 28, 59, 84, 115, 116, 117, 149–63, 179, 180, 185, 188, 189
Russia, 26, 27, 28, 192

Salamis, island of, *141*, 144
Sanskrit, 16, 22, 23, 24, *25*, 71, 90, 95, 97
Sargon, King, 42
Sarmatians, 183–85, 191
Sassanids, 116, 117
Scandinavia, 14, 19
Schliemann, Heinrich, 131
Scythians, 17, 26, 107, 111, 171, 176, 183, 184, 186
Sea People, 22, 56, 152
Semitic languages, 62
Shiva, 102–03
Sicily, *151*, 192
Sinai, *65*, 67
Slavic languages, 23, *25*
Socrates, 145–46
Solon, 142
Sophocles, 138, 145
Spain, 153, *157*, 167, 177, 190
Sparta, 133, 141, *141*, 142–43, 145, 146
Stonehenge, 196, 197
Sumerians, 17, 24, 36–43, 93, 141
Sybaris, 151, *157*
Syracuse, *141*, 151, 152, *157*
Syria, 18, 48, *49*, 56, 65, *65*, 69, 70, 71, 143, *157*
Syro-Palestine, 61, 62, 63, 64, *65*, 66, 67, 68, 69, 70, 77

Tacitus, 180–81, 182, 185, 190, 191, 193
Teutons (Germans), *19*, 22, 179–82, 185, 187, 190–91, 193
Thebes, Egypt, *78*, 79
Thebes, Greece, *141*, 144, 146
Themistocles, 145
Thermopylae, *109*, 144
Theseus, legend of, 127–28, 129
Thespis, 137

Thor, 16, 181
Thrace, 26, *157*
Thucydides, 140
Thutmose I, 68, 80
Thutmose III, 69, 80, 81
Thutmose IV, 70
Tiber River, 149, *151*, 152
Tigris River, *12*, 17, *19*, 33, *34*, 36, 42, 43, 47, *49*, *65*, 66, *109*
Trajan, Emperor, 157, 188
Troy, *49*, 50, 70, *124*, 131
Tutankhamon, 82

Ugarit, 61, *65*, 67
Umma, *34*, 42
Upper Egypt, 74, *78*
Ur, *34*, 38, 39, 41, 43, 48
Urnfield People, 169–71, *170*, 172
Urukagina, King, 42

Van, Lake, *34*, 61, 64, 70
Vandals, 187
Varuna, 16, 69, 91, 97, 106
Vedas, 95–96, 97, 98, 102, 106
Vergil, 159
Vespasian, Emperor, 157
Vikings, 19, 191–93, 199
Vishnu, 102
Visigoths, 185, 187, 190

Wassuggani, 68, 70
Wheel, invention of, 17
Wheeler, Sir Mortimer, 103

Xenophon, 146
Xerxes, 113, 144, 145

Zagros Mountains, *12*, 32, 33, *34*, 42, 44, 48, *49*, 52, 106
Zeus, 16, 128, 158
Ziggurat of Ur, 39, 43
Ziu, 16, 181, 192
Zoroaster, 105–10 *passim*, 115, 116

About the author

OLIVIA VLAHOS was born in Houston, Texas. She attended the University of Texas, concentrating in anthropology and drama. Having received her B.A. degree, she acted professionally for a time, and later returned to the university to do graduate work in anthropology. Subsequently, she received her Master of Arts degree from Sarah Lawrence College.

Mrs. Vlahos lives with her husband, playwright John Vlahos, and their three children in Westport, Connecticut. She is presently teaching at the Norwalk Community College in Norwalk, Connecticut, where she is offering courses in introductory anthropology and African area studies, the subjects treated in her first two books, *Human Beginnings* and *African Beginnings*.